FIRST TIME AROUND

A Novel By
Michael J. Bellito

Strategic Book Group

Copyright © 2011

All rights reserved—Michael J. Bellito

No part of this book may be reproduced or transmitted in any form or by any means, graphic, electronic, or mechanical, including photocopying, recording, taping, or by any information storage retrieval system, without the permission, in writing, of the publisher.

Strategic Book Group
P.O. Box 333
Durham CT 06422
www.StrategicBookClub.com

Design: Dedicated Business Solutions, Inc. (www.netdbs.com)

ISBN: 978-1-61204-348-7

To my children, Matt and Joy, whose lives are a constant inspiration to me.

Special thanks to:

Erin Brooks, the best grammar-girl in the world.

And to:

Patty and Emil Misichko, for plowing through the first draft and providing encouragement along the way.

Anita Thies, for help with the French language.

First Time Around is a work of fiction. Any resemblance to any persons (living or dead), situations, or events is completely coincidental.

M. J. Bellito

1

John Belson wasn't the least bit scared. Why should he be? After all, he was an eighth grader—top dog, big cheese, king of the hill. He knew the building, Miller Junior High School, with its endless rows of neat lockers, polished tile floors, and oversized classrooms, built to usher in the 1960s, when baby boomers were coming of age and suburban schools were sprouting up like spring grass, every one of the edifices cleaner and shinier and more expansive than its ancient predecessor. He knew the ins and outs of the maze—the corridors that were passageways to the art and music rooms, the mini-stairway to the boys' locker room, the secret shortcut behind the stage that assured a spot at the front of the lunch line. Despite all this, he felt queasy as the bus screeched to a stop in the circle drive at the main entrance. An empty, hollow ache gnawed at his stomach. But it wasn't fear that assailed him. John Belson was lonely.

Stepping slowly off the bus and shuffling along with his head down, John was soon swept up by the surging stream of hormones and carried like baggage into the building. He followed the restless bodies up the wide staircase and headed toward where he was certain his locker would be—in alphabetical order in the eighth-grade wing.

And there it was, number 865, near the boys' room. John deftly twirled through the set of numbers scrawled on the scrap of paper in his hand. He pulled hard on the handle, and the locker clanked open. He swung it back and forth on its hinges several times and slammed it shut. There was no coat to hang up in early September, and textbooks hadn't been issued yet. To impress the teachers, John would carry his three-subject notebooks, pens, and No. 2 pencils to each of his classes today.

The noise around him grew louder as more kids shot out of the stairwell into the hallway. Standing with his back to his locker, he watched with envy the backslapping boys and squealing girls welcome each other back from the short summer. How long would it be until someone—anyone—acknowledged his presence?

"Hey, Belson, you dork!"

Finally, a friendly face. John knew Bill Dobbs from Little League. A big, likable kid with a dark crew cut, Bill was a workhorse on the mound, and opponents feared his wicked fastball. The two boys had also teamed up in seventh-grade shop class to help each other finish a project. The most difficult part of creating the homemade bongos had been the last task—the stretching and tacking of the wet skins so they fit snugly over the edges of the wood. John recalled Bill's impassioned pleas to: "Pull hard, Belson, if you want our bongos to look good."

John zigzagged through the mass of bodies—a mix of cologne and perfume—and approached the large boy's locker. The last time they had seen each other was at the championship game in July, a 6-5 defeat.

"Hi, Bill. How was your summer?"

"Better than yours, I'm sure. While you were at home picking your nose and watching your pathetic Cubs lose every game, I was at camp in Wisconsin."

"How was it?"

"Mostly okay, I guess. Some kid drowned though. His parents had to come and get the body, which was lousy. We all had to stay in the next day. I think the counselors were trying to figure out what to do. But we got to finish out the week. Anyway, I made out with Laurie Jenkins on the last night. We snuck away from the campfire when everyone was singing dopey songs and went off into the woods."

John's eyes grew large. Laurie Jenkins had the biggest pair in the eighth grade. "You liar."

Bill looked offended. "I never lie about titty."

A loud clang, followed by yelling and banging, interrupted their banter. Down the hall, a sixth grader had mistakenly wandered into the wrong wing and was now fighting for air and sanity within the close confines of a musty locker.

"Serves him right," Bill remarked. "The little twerp shouldn't be up here in the first place."

John felt a twinge of sadness for the prisoner but said nothing. An adult would appear soon enough and release him.

"So, who's your LASS teacher?" Bill asked.

LASS stood for Language Arts/Social Studies. The class met thrice daily during the nine-period schedule. One's LASS teacher was also considered to be the homeroom "counselor" and therefore responsible for most parent contact.

"Mr. Schwartz," John said.

"I've heard he's okay. I've got Mrs. Danforth." Bill's expressive face scrunched up. "She's a real witch. They say she'll whack you one for no good reason, just for lookin' out the window or something."

The pain in John's stomach struck again. "Too bad we're not together."

This was a heartfelt sentiment. John liked Bill's quick humor and laid-back attitude. Shop class the past year had been a riot, Bill producing dirty jokes with assembly-line speed and precision timing until his captive listeners blew snot from their noses. Mr. Black, who ran his classes like a warden, more than once stifled the boys' laughter with a glower across the bustling room, seemingly confused that anyone would not take wood seriously. During one memorable staredown, a jigsaw removed the top half of his left pinkie, which bothered him not at all.

"Are we together for even one class?" John unfolded his schedule and held it out for Bill to see.

Bill pulled his own schedule from his pocket and did a rapid comparison. "Nope. Oh, wait, there's lunch." All the eighth graders ate together during fifth period. "Other than that, you'll just have to play with yourself all day. And now, farewell, my lad, I'm off to greener pastures. Hey, Cindy!"

John was alone again. His eyes followed Bill's frame as the friendly boy loped down the hall in the direction of Cindy Sandlund, a petite girl with blond hair and green eyes. Glancing back down toward his hands, he studied his schedule.

First period. Art with Mr. Robinson. John, one of the most uncreative children in God's universe, hated art. He tried hard, but nothing ever looked right when he was finished. Nor did he understand art's basic concepts, such as perspective. He drew the lines for the bowling lanes straight because lanes *were* straight, and no art teacher's explanation of how they had to slant inward closer to the pins would ever prove satisfactory to his practical mind.

The next two periods were LASS, with French thrown in three times a week, followed by gym and lunch. This was good, thought John. At least he didn't have gym *after* lunch when the cafeteria meatloaf hadn't had time to settle. Next came science, then back to LASS, math, and finally, study hall.

The best aspect of study hall was that the eighth graders could sign up during that time period for "special classes" ranging from choir to sports to chess club to biology. In other words, something for everybody.

John looked around one more time at the barely contained chaos, the introvert's noisy nightmare. The thing was that, until last year, John had been more of an extrovert. Sixth grade had witnessed an awakening of his soul and spirit. There had been new friends, and not just guys. Co-ed "mixers" had introduced him to girls, who laughed at his jokes while teaching him to move to the sexually charged dances of the day. John, in turn, became more outgoing; he even dared to envision a future marriage to Debbie, Monica, Carol, or Wendy.

But that had been at Oliver Wendell Holmes Junior High across town, before the meddlers decided a second school needed to be built to keep up with exploding enrollment. They condemned John's block to be included in the revised map area for the new building. Without moving, John was suddenly separated from all the people he liked and trusted. Only a few of his childhood playmates who lived on his street accompanied him to his new school. The rest of the pack was made up of strangers, none of whom laughed at John's clever imitations of teachers, cared if he liked to play chess or read the works of Edgar Allan Poe and Sir Arthur Conan Doyle, or willingly picked him for their team in gym class.

Even his grades, which had always been stellar, divebombed. His teachers no longer perceived him as bright and self-motivated, and notices home were no longer "commendations." Rather, they were "failures." Increased weight brought athletic struggles as well, and the cycle of defeat repeated itself as John took comfort in eating whenever it was convenient.

Passing quickly through the crowded halls, John slid noiselessly into the art room and sat down on a stool near the window. He scanned the faces. Why did none of them seem familiar? He had attended Miller Junior High for a full year, hadn't he?

The bell rang.

"Welcome to your first thirteen-week class—art." Mr. Robinson hadn't changed since last year. Horned-rimmed bifocals and a moustache under thinning brown hair. A green cardigan sweater with neat patches on the elbows. A polite smile that made him seem friendly. Until one got to know him, thought John, remembering the "D" the teacher had given his seventh-grade clay project—an alligator who had, unfortunately, been left too long in the kiln, causing one of its legs to fall off.

"After this class, you will all move on to music and then practical arts—shop for the boys and home economics for the girls."

John didn't mind music, but he hated shop class almost as much as art. Truth be told, he would have preferred making scrambled eggs and bundt cakes to tie racks and bongos.

"Our first projects this year will be clay sculptures. You will shape them, bake them in the kiln, and paint them."

Oh, please, not again, thought John.

"After I call roll, you may get up from your seats and look at—but do not touch—some of the excellent pieces from last year displayed on the shelf to my left. They are truly amazing."

Mr. Robinson paused momentarily during his effusive praise. Most likely, none of the potential Picassos who'd created these modern-art masterpieces would go on to immortality in the nebulous world of art, but that didn't matter. They were prototypes, and John's class had better strive to match their perfection.

"Now, to more mundane matters. Please say 'here' if you are present. Darlene Adams."

"Here."

"Barbara Anderson."

"Here."

"John Bel—"

The door crashed open. A tall, dark-haired boy with a wide grin burst into the classroom. The boys looked surprised; the girls looked excited; Mr. Robinson looked bewildered.

"May I help you?"

"Yes, I'm Jeff Womack," the boy said, "and I'm sorry I'm late to your class. I'm new to this school, and I couldn't find the art room."

Mr. Robinson snatched the schedule from the boy's hand. "Hmm . . . well, you're in the right place. Please take a seat, and don't come late again."

Right, thought John. As if the poor kid came late on purpose so he could be humiliated in front of a group of snobs and bullies. But the funny thing was that the new boy didn't seem a bit fazed. He smiled politely at the grim-faced teacher, said, "Thank you, sir," and walked to a seat on the opposite side of the classroom. Two girls giggled as he glided past them, dirty thoughts in their heads. For a flash, the boy's demeanor reminded John of someone truly dangerous, like Shane in Jack Schaefer's classic novel.

When the bell rang to dismiss them, the class moved en masse. There was never time for anything more than a quick slurp of water or a pit stop for a pee before the haggard cattle were driven by instinct to their various destinations. John allowed himself a moment's indecision—should he go out of his way to help the new boy find his next class? No, then he would be late himself, he reasoned. And besides, Jeff—was that his name?—had already disappeared into the herd.

Mr. Schwartz, wearing a white shirt, thin black tie, and the tightest pants John had ever seen, greeted his LASS class warmly as the boys and girls filed into the room and took their seats. His reputation was one of a hard, but fair, instructor who took his job of molding lazy eighth graders into high-school-ready students very seriously. Except when Miss Parras came in three times weekly during third period for a half hour of French, Mr. Schwartz would teach this class fifteen periods a week.

The room, near John's locker, was large and well lit, sun streaming in through the bank of windows that looked down on the street below. Each of the fifteen tables had two chairs, a grand total of thirty seats. As John glanced around at the faces, he recognized some from last year. Again, however, most seemed unfamiliar. He was inwardly delighted to glance across the aisle and see Nancy Olson, an attractive blond with blue eyes and a sweet smile, but she looked through him as if he wasn't there and waved to a girl seated near the door.

John's heart sank. He turned slowly in his chair and gazed blankly at the nearly full classroom behind him. Twenty-nine seats were taken; the only empty one sat beside him. As his peers had entered the classroom, not one had chosen to sit at his table.

A wave of sadness overwhelmed him. He fought back tears, knowing this would only worsen his situation. Unless Mr. Schwartz changed their seats, he would be alone, isolated on an island while an ocean of laughter and warmth swelled up around him. Surrendering to his fate, he turned and listened to his teacher's voice monotonously calling the roll.

Without warning, the door crashed open.

2

"And why, exactly, did you think it was a good idea to put a pig's head in Margie Bruce's locker?"

It had come to this. John Belson and his new friend Jeff Womack were seated in the assistant principal's carpeted office for their third visit in a month, and Mr. Carver did not look happy.

***

The first trip had come about because John and Jeff found out they had something in common: they loved to laugh out loud at stupid things. During the first few weeks of school, every time Mr. Schwartz turned to write something on the chalkboard, Jeff pulled out an outrageous caricature that he had drawn of someone they knew. In true Thomas Nast-style satire, no one was spared. Teachers, of course, were the most frequent targets. There was Mr. Robinson, paint-speckled face and clay up to his elbows, saying, "Art is life. Well, *my* boring life anyway." Mr. Schwartz was shown from behind, bending over to pick up a piece of chalk, the bulge of his wallet looking more like a safe stuck in his back pocket, his skin-tight pants splitting to the sound of "Rrriiip." He was yelling, "I feel a breeze in here! Did someone open a window?" And Mr. Dumpmore, their paunchy gym teacher, was drawn covered in blood, bodies at his feet, holding up a hard rubber ball and sneering, "I just love dodge ball."

True friendship never happens overnight. Jeff had taken the vacant seat next to John on that first day of school and had been nice to him. That alone had given John hope. As the weeks progressed, the proximity to each other in LASS and a few other classes—their schedules were identical—had bonded them like glue. By the time Jeff slid the cartoon of their math teacher Miss Stuart across the table toward John, causing him to snort out an aborted laugh, it was understood by everyone that they were best friends.

Mr. Schwartz spun around. "Let's have it! Hand it over now!"

Jeff picked up the paper and reluctantly relinquished it.

The teacher, frowning, studied the demented drawing. Miss Stuart's glasses were pushed down to the end of her nose, her mouth was set in a tight scowl, and her more-than-ample hips dominated her dwarfish frame. The balloon over her head read: "$1 + 1 = 2$, but I've never had a screw!"

"Oh, dear. This is inappropriate." Mr. Schwartz's demeanor shifted between disappointment and downright anger. There was a rumor that he was dating the shrewish mathematician. He stared down at the boys. "What am I going to do with you two? For the past month, you've done nothing but act like jackasses."

The class tittered.

"Quiet!" His mind made up, Mr. Schwartz walked rapidly to his desk, sat down and wrote a quick note, stapled the offensive artwork to it, and spoke. "John, Jeff, I want you to take this to Mr. Carver's office. He'll know what to do with you."

John was petrified. He had never, ever, in his entire school career, been sent to the office to be disciplined. Jeff was nonchalant, as cool as always. "Big deal," he said, ambling down the vacant hallway a few steps ahead of his terrified partner-in-crime. "At my last school, they whipped us for less than this." Jeff's parents, in an attempt to control his behavior, had enrolled him for two years in a military school in Wisconsin. He stopped and bent over, gesturing as if to pull down his trousers. "Wanna see my scars?"

John jumped backward, visibly upset.

"I'm just shittin' you. C'mon, don't worry. It'll be all right."

And it was. Mr. Carver was a gentle, soft-spoken man, the antithesis of what the boys expected. A typical assistant principal was a stern second-in-command, acting as both mouthpiece and assassin for the principal, whom students never saw. But he just sat calmly in an oversized chair at an oaken desk, carefully reading the note from Mr. Schwartz. Then, he looked at the drawing. His eyes twinkled briefly, and he stifled a laugh, drawing a fist to his mouth and coughing instead. Composing himself, he said, "Listen up."

After lecturing the boys about how hurtful it would be if Miss Stuart ever laid eyes on the mean-spirited caricature, he sent them back to LASS with a warning: the next time they were sent to his office, they would stay after school for a week and clean desks until they dropped. Was that clear?

The second incident was less complicated. No one's freedom of artistic expression was being denied. Besides the occasional spitball, there had been no more horsing around in Mr. Schwartz's class. He had separated the troublemakers by "switching seats." But Mr. Robinson's class was altogether different, a perfect setting for random mischief.

The art room, in its very purpose, demanded freedom of movement. The typical period saw girls and boys dressed in clay- or paint-covered smocks bustling about from supply drawer to easels to kiln, a Marx Brothers merry-go-round of motion. Gauguins, Renoirs, Van Goghs—all of them desperately trying to sculpt, to draw, to paint. Trying to at least finish their misshapen clay swans and deformed ballerinas by the due date. Or else Mr. Robinson, frowning and "cluck-clucking," would brand them with a "D" and a sad, "I'm afraid there won't be a spot on the shelf for your project on Parent Night."

"Hey, John, look at this." On Jeff's leg rested a paper bag, stiffened by whatever was inside it. Glancing around the room, he cautiously withdrew an object from the sack. It was long and narrow and silver, and John had no idea what it was.

"What is it?"

"It's a cattle prod." Jeff had grown up in Iowa. "I suppose you Chicago boys have never seen one."

"What does it do?"

Jeff snickered. "What does it do? Well, you see, when old Bossy don't move, you come up behind her and stick this here end up against her fat ass, and 'moooo,' she takes off runnin' like the Devil's after her."

John's face grew dark. His eyebrows scrunched downward over his nose. "Oh, no. You're not planning on . . ."

Jeff grinned.

"Who?"

"Brenda Wiggins."

Jeff had only been at Miller for a month, but he already knew who Brenda Wiggins was. Everyone did. And outside of her snobbish social sphere, no one liked her. Last year, she had taken out her two main rivals for the last spot on the cheerleading squad by serving them homemade cupcakes an hour before the tryouts as a friendly gesture of "esprit de corps." The cramping and diarrhea that followed was a balm compared to the utter humiliation and worthlessness the girls felt on being deprived of their one chance to follow their junior high dreams. Scorned by their peers, they would spend the rest of their school years as "wannabees," looking in at the pristine snow globe from the outside.

Because many of the teachers used alphabetical order to determine their seating charts, Jeff and Brenda sat next to each other in several classes. True, he was handsome, even charming, but he was new and seemed to be drawn to loser kids like Belson. And she already had plenty of unwanted attention from love-struck boys, so she ignored him. Jeff doubted she ever would again.

She was on the other side of the room, putting the finishing touches on a self-portrait of a cheerleader in action. The painting showed the girl suspended in mid-air, head askew, blond hair splayed to one side, legs bent at the knees as the bright white tennis shoes kicked out behind her. Originally, Brenda had sketched herself doing the splits, arms and legs shooting out to the sides, fingers straining to touch toes, skirt shooting upward, and just a hint of white cotton panties. Mr. Robinson, beads of sweat forming on his temples, had blushed at the concept and suggested—no, insisted upon—a revised pose. For once, perspective seemed too real for him.

Jeff and John approached Brenda from the rear. They had agreed that, since there could be only one strike, they would act together. So, at the last minute, each boy placed one warm hand on the smooth metal pole. It was over quickly.

The simultaneous sounds of the electric "ZAP" and Brenda's painful shriek echoed around the room. All work ceased. Some, searching for the source of the clamor, turned in time to see Brenda's quivering body pitch forward into the easel, the still-wet painting pressing up against her chest and face as everything tumbled to the cold tile floor.

By the end of that week, every desk in Miller Junior High School had been scrubbed clean.

And now, only weeks later, the misbehaving youths had completed the trifecta. As eighth graders, they had been allowed to sign up for an elective during their ninth-period study hall. These lasted about six weeks. John had tried to get into chess club, but it was full, so he settled for basic biology; his friend Jeff did likewise.

Mr. Schneider, gaunt and bespectacled, might have been Mr. Robinson's queer twin. But, unlike the art teacher, he had no passion for his subject. His droning voice explained the science of searching for amoeba, euglena, and paramecium under a microscope as if reading directions to assemble a lamp. A few weeks into the session, he stood before the group and lectured, a painfully common occurrence.

"Now that we have studied the central nervous and digestive systems of the pig via our diagrams, we will proceed—in pairs—to actually dissect an embryo of this animal." One or two girls squealed in distress. "When you arrive each day," he continued, hand poised over a gigantic jar, "you will lift the top from this container and remove your pig, each of which is tagged on the right foreleg with a specific number that you will commit to memory. Do not, I repeat, do *not* place your bare hand into the vat to take out your pig, but rather use these tongs to extricate it from the herd. The reason for this is the formaldehyde in which the unborn pigs rest. Not only does it emit an extremely pungent odor, but it can also cause irritation of the eyes, nose, throat, and skin. At the conclusion of each period, you will place your specimens back into their sleeping quarters." He paused briefly to allow for laughter. There was none.

A week went by. Bodies were split open; entrails were revealed. "Gross" was a frequently uttered word, and Betsy Mires threw up. Mr. Schneider was content to pace the room and occasionally comment on the surgery. After the digestive tract had been explored, students were encouraged to pick apart their pig's skull in a circular fashion to expose its brain.

This is when Jeff hit upon a bad idea. John, always the follower, agreed that it would indeed be a big surprise if sweet little Margie Bruce opened her locker after school and discovered a grinning pig's head, brain sticking out the top. With the brazen attitude the boys had developed over the last month, the pig was decapitated, and its headless torso was unceremoniously dumped back into the tub on the way out the door. Mr. Schneider, taking in the bright metamorphosis of leaves outside the windows, never even glanced in the boys' direction. The rest of the plot eventually became the stuff of legend.

***

"Can you just answer that one question for me?" repeated a more-than-a-little-irritated Mr. Carver.

John shifted uncomfortably in his chair. He looked nervously around the room to avoid eye contact with Mr. Carver and realized how familiar this setting had become in recent weeks.

"No? Then let me put it another way, boys. What in God's name were you thinking?"

This time, even Jeff realized in retrospect that they had gone too far. "Well, sir," he ventured, "I guess we weren't thinking." He wanted to add, "But if you'd only seen Margie's face . . ." and thought better of it.

"I see. Well, I suppose this is a clear-cut case of 'the third time's the charm.' I'm going to call your parents up to see if that doesn't straighten you out."

Both boys sagged deeper into their upholstered chairs. In this era, one maxim applied: guilty at school, guilty at home. There was no: "Now, John, before your father beats you, perhaps we should hear *your* side of the story."

"And furthermore, you are being removed from biology and placed back in study hall. You are not going to be given extra privileges such as these while your reckless behavior continues unabated."

John spoke for the first time. "Sir, will I be allowed to sign up for chess club next session?"

"No. You most certainly will not. Until you have proven to me beyond a shadow of a doubt that you can be trusted, you . . ." Mr. Carver hesitated in mid-sentence. He smiled almost kindly at the boys. "Don't you understand? It's a matter of maturity, of growing up. Mark my words: someday very soon you will look with wonder upon these same young girls that you now torment. Simply put, boys, someday you will fall in love."

Was this possible? thought John. He suddenly remembered how nice the girls at his other school had been to him. How they had patiently taught him to master the twist and the pony. How they had laughed at his "knock-knock" jokes and his imitations of Barney Fife. Maybe Mr. Carver was right. Margie Bruce had done nothing to harm him. Why had it seemed so cool to frighten her?

John stole a glance at his despondent friend beside him. Instead of acting like fifth graders, he wondered, perhaps they should abandon their pirate ways, casting into the sea's current their nasty cartoons, electric cattle prods, and putrid pigs' heads. Perhaps they should become civilized, blending smoothly into the social swirl of eighth grade. Perhaps they should date.

3

"Riiiiiing . . . Ri—"

Click.

"I can't do it. I just can't do it." John buried his face in a pillow. Thirty seconds later, he pulled it away, using it to wipe sweat from his forehead and hands. He looked helplessly into the exasperated eyes of his friend.

"*Why* can't you do it?"

"Because I can't."

"Not a reason. You can and you will." Jeff paused while he considered an alternative battle plan. "Do you want me to call her for you?"

"Her" was Nancy Olson, the blue-eyed blond who sat across the aisle from John in LASS. She was the prettiest girl John had ever known. And he thought, as Mr. Carver had suggested, that he might even have fallen in love with her. Once or twice he had caught himself staring over at her, his eyes transfixed on one soft, white leg crossed atop the other, bouncing along to the rhythm of her joyous imagination. At times, she would stop the kicking motion, her leg taut and still, and slowly twirl her saddle shoe in a circle. Then, his head would revolve in a similar motion. Once, she'd caught him watching and smiled at him, and his stomach turned to water.

"No, I don't want you to call her. What would you say? Hello, Nancy, this is Jeff Womack calling on behalf of John Belson the yellow-belly. He wants to ask you out, but he's a chicken who can't work up the nerve."

The last part of this tirade was spat out with a certain self-loathing as John realized he spoke the truth. He was afraid. Afraid to call a person he saw in class every single day. Afraid to suggest that she and her friend Mary Lou Mason might enjoy an evening of bowling in the escort of two young gentlemen this coming Friday.

For that was the plan. A double date. Safe, secure, responsible. Paranoid parents who wouldn't allow their virgin daughters to go out on a date with a single boy for fear of what might transpire in the back row of the local movie theatre gleefully permitted the young girls to engage in the social interaction of a foursome. It was a surefire way for a boy to appear wholesome. And, if he ran out of things to say, his buddy was there to pull him out of the quicksand. And all John had to accomplish was the single most difficult task in the world for an eighth-grade boy: call the girl and ask her.

"Look," said Jeff, "when I asked Mary Lou this afternoon—need I remind you that she said it sounded like great fun?—I might have let slip that you would be calling Nancy tonight."

"You *what*?"

"So she's probably waiting by the phone."

"Oh, Lord, what have you done to me?"

"C'mon. Pick up the phone. Remember, be polite but firm; no small talk. Be sure to tell her that Mary Lou already said yes. And my dad will pick them up and drop them off back home. I'm telling you, she'll be thrilled. Girls always are when you pay attention to them."

John stretched out his shaking hand and gripped the black receiver. He looked once more at his friend for support.

"C'mon. It'll be over in a minute."

And it was.

"Hello." It was Nancy's older sister.

"Hello. May I please speak to Nancy?"

"Nancy! Phone!"

The next twenty seconds were the longest in John's life. While he waited, he considered giving up, hanging up, and throwing up.

"It's for you. It's a boy."

John could clearly hear the mocking tone in her voice as she teased her younger sister. Unfortunately, Nancy's whispered reactions were also audible.

"Who is it?"

"Who's calling, please?"

"Uh, John Belson."

"It's John Belson."

"Noooo."

"One minute, please."

"Tell him I'm not home."

The silent tug-of-war between siblings became visible in John's mind. There was the older sister, holding out the phone in a taunting "this-I've-got-to-see" manner while the defiant younger one hopelessly attempted to assert her fledgling independence by crossing her arms and scowling back at her tormentor's saccharin smile. Birth order had long ago determined the winner.

"Hello."

"Hi," John squeaked. "Nancy? This is John Belson. Um, I was wondering if you'd like to go bowling with me this Friday night. We'd be going with Jeff Womack and Mary Lou Mason. Jeff's dad will drive."

And that was that. He hadn't faltered even momentarily in his delivery. He had achieved the unachievable. Jeff smiled at him and gave him a thumbs-up.

"I'm sorry. I can't. My father won't let me go out with boys." The lie was uttered with such conviction, such sweet sincerity, that John almost believed it, desperately wanted to believe it. But as the line went dead, he remembered her impassioned pleas to her sister. She had not even wanted to speak to him.

"Bye." John's voice echoed softly in the void. His emasculation was complete.

***

The next day in school, John avoided eye contact with Nancy. After the neat rejection, it would have been pointless. John had, of course, spilled his guts to Jeff, who listened with astonishment and then dubbed Nancy "Lady Lucifer." Ever the optimist, Jeff promised John that, with two days yet to go, he would help him land a date.

It so happened that Mary Lou Mason had a cousin named Lisa who lived in the city and supposedly had a great personality. The deal was sealed when Mary Lou told Jeff that she'd arranged for Lisa to sleep over at her house on Friday night. John found out about it after the fact.

"No," he stated in an unusual display of anger. "I am not going out with Mary Lou's ugly cousin. I don't care what kind of personality she has. Maybe you should take both of them out. You know, improve your reputation at school."

Considering how helpful Jeff had been in trying to bolster John's attempt at a love life, the last comment seemed especially hurtful, designed to suggest that Jeff was only out for himself.

"Suit yourself, ass-face. I guess we'll both be sitting home then. 'Cause I'm not going without you. We can watch 'Rawhide' together."

John was genuinely touched. He had never had a friend who was willing to sacrifice so much for him, and he suddenly felt selfish and ashamed. "Okay, fine. We'll all go."

"That's my boy," said a smiling Jeff.

"Hey . . ." John halted. "Thanks. I mean it."

"What are friends for? My dad and I'll pick you up at seven o'clock. Then we'll go get the girls. Be ready."

***

John, Jeff, Mary Lou, and Lisa—who was not a bit ugly—sat quietly in the dark. Stuck in the Pontiac's large back seat with the two girls, John pressed himself tightly up against the door and tried not to breathe too loudly. Whenever Jeff made their dates giggle with a funny remark, John laughed along, desperately trying to fit in. But it seemed hopeless. Bouncing along, he wondered if Gil Favor and Rowdy Yates were having any trouble with rustlers.

In this era, there was no cooler place to hang out than the bowling alley. Young teens were seduced by the smoke-filled venue, a lively spot to yuk it up with friends while chugging bottles of Coca-Cola to the ceaseless background noise of crashing pins. Parents loved it too, mostly because it was well lit, crowded, and supervised—a roller rink without the risks. And besides, it could be argued that it was a type of training in a semi-athletic skill. Not as strenuous as running bases or swimming the length of a pool, but arduous enough to work up a mild sweat and exercise rarely used muscles. It was true that the adult regulars, with flab spilling over their belts and wet stains creeping from beneath their armpits and breasts, looked nothing like professional athletes. But youngsters regarded them as an integral part of the sideshow and seldom, if ever, saw their own futures staring back at them through the bloodshot eyes of one-too-many Pabst Blue Ribbon Beers.

The foursome piled out of the car and headed through the glass doors of Mount Pleasant owling—the neon "B" was out again. The boys rented the pairs of shoes and were assigned a lane.

"Cool," blurted out John in an attempt to show the girls he could speak. "Lane 14. Ernie Banks' number."

Mary Lou shot Lisa an I'm-sorry-I-promise-I'll-make-it-up-to-you look as she bent down to lace her shoes.

Then, like the village idiot, John looked at Jeff and said enthusiastically, "Why don't we grab our balls?"

Of course, at that very moment, there was near silence across all sixteen lanes of the gigantic room. Not one sphere spun across hardwood; not one explosion echoed from a hard-thrown strike; not one belly laugh, belch, or swear word came forth from the mouth of a fellow patron. It seemed to John as if the universe had been stifled—planets suspended in motion, shooting stars stilled in the sky. He looked over to gage the girls' reaction to his faux pas.

He expected to see horror-stricken stares of disbelief and disgust before they walked over to the phone booth and called Mary Lou's dad to come pick them up. "Daddy, can you come get us? Lisa's date—you know, that John Belson boy—is talking dirty. I should have known better than to ask her to go out with the little creep."

Instead, John saw only the tops of their heads as they put the dramatic finishing touch on their laces, the always fashionable double bow. Mary Lou looked up and said without a touch of sarcasm, "Well, shall we go pick out our balls?"

John's guardian angel smiled down at him.

"Why didn't you just say, 'So, why don't you put your hands down our pants?'" whispered Jeff as they stood at the racks.

"Sorry," mumbled John.

"Well, what do you think of Lisa?"

"She's nice. Kinda cute."

"Good. I'm glad you find her attractive. Now, just relax and make some normal conversation with her, and I'm sure we'll all have fun."

The girls returned with appropriately colorful—pink and baby blue—bowling balls, and the first game began. A city girl, Lisa was a top-notch bowler. John, a better-than-average bowler himself, was both surprised and impressed.

"You're really good," he commented as he marked yet another spare for her in the sixth frame.

"Thanks," she said with a quick smile. "I live right down the street from an alley. I guess I've spent some time there."

"So, what's it like? Living in the city, I mean?"

"Well, it's different. Everything's busier, more crowded." Laughing, she said, "There are fifty-seven kids in my English class."

"What?"

"Pretty crazy, huh? Mary tells me you guys have half as many."

"Where do you fit 'em all?"

"The classrooms are huge, real long and narrow. If you sit in the back, you're about a million miles away from the teacher."

"Yes! A turkey!" Jeff's voice came crashing back at them. Chest out and knees bent, he strutted toward the scorer's table. "Gobble-gobble. Mark that down, John!"

Mary Lou laughed loudly at his antics.

John had to admit he was having fun. He looked up to see Jeff giving pointers to his date. Standing close behind Mary Lou, he was instructing her how to release the ball just so. His right hand was on top of hers; his left rested gently on her waist.

Lisa giggled softly beside him. "Mary's actually a very good bowler."

John suddenly saw Jeff not as a handsome, popular stud, but as a helpless puddle of pudding waiting to be devoured by a crafty sex kitten.

While the free play continued, John stole a sideways glance at Lisa. She really was cute. Brunette, creamy complexion, straight white teeth—she must have worn braces when she was younger—and black-framed glasses. Most guys were turned off by girls who wore glasses, but John liked the added dimension to her pretty face, the brown eyes secreted behind them. Besides, he wore glasses too, since fifth grade, another reason kids made fun of him.

The first game ended with the boys' scores only slightly higher than the girls'. Lisa had been leading everyone until the tenth frame, when she unexpectedly served up two gutter balls in a row. John thought it a suspicious event. After the game, the girls bolted to the bathroom. The boys went to buy Cokes.

"Mary Lou's a pretty good bowler," John said with a smirk.

"She's okay, I guess. You may have noticed I gave her some pointers."

"Sure."

"What's that supposed to mean?"

"Nothing."

Back together, the foursome sipped from the bottles and prepared to begin the second game.

"Why don't we play teams this time?" suggested Jeff. "Mary Lou and me against you two. Highest combined score wins."

"Good idea!"

Bad idea. Competition brought out the worst in the guys, and what had been a carefree evening of light banter turned into a hostile, win-or-else environment with taunts and barbs being slung back and forth. Scores were double- and triple-checked.

"Excuse me, but there were only three pins left standing, not four. Change that."

"No, you're wrong. I watched them get swept up. There was another pin behind the ones in front that you couldn't see."

"Not true. I could see everything, and there were only three."

"You didn't see anything. You were walking back with your head down."

The climax, such as it was, came in the final frame, the outcome still very much in doubt. Jeff, in a rage after hurling a gutter ball, swung his arm backward to begin his second shot, and the ball slipped out of his sweaty grasp and crashed onto the hardwood floor behind him.

Steaming, he snatched the ball up, turned around, and once again prepared to bowl.

"Hey, meathead!" yelled John. "What're you doing?"

"What does it look like I'm doing? I'm taking my second shot!"

"That *was* your second shot!"

"Was not. The ball slipped."

"Was too, cheater!"

Jeff paused. "What did you call me?"

"You heard me."

The girls cringed.

Before John knew it, his face was being driven into the floor as Jeff tightened the grip around his neck. John responded by slamming his elbow three or four times into Jeff's ribcage. Thankfully, two big guys in the next lane broke up the impromptu wrestling match before either boy got hurt. "What's-a-madder wid you kids? You nuts or what?"

That about covered it.

The silent ride home was interrupted only once by Jeff's taciturn father, who asked politely, "So, did you kids have fun?"

Lisa, whom John would never see again, scrambled out of the car with her cousin. Turning back, she said, "Thank you for a lovely evening."

The sad thing was that she sounded sincere. Who knew? Maybe her city dates ended in bloodshed. Anyway, John fumed, they would have had a fine time if wacko Jeff hadn't lost it. Instead, his once-in-a-lifetime dream date had been shattered.

Slamming the car door behind him, John stomped into his house and—ignoring his parents' questions—went straight to bed. Alone in the dark, sick with a bad case of bowling alley blues, he reflected on the evening's events. And though it was easy to blame Jeff for what had happened, he understood that he had also been at fault.

Then, John pushed the ugly incident out of his mind and thought about Lisa. He thought about how pretty she had turned out to be and felt a twinge of remorse for thinking she would be ugly. He thought about how sweet she was and how easy it would be to fall in love with her and get married someday and have a family together and . . .

A warm feeling engulfed his entire body, and he drifted off into an ocean of pleasant dreams.

4

It started off like any other Friday. And there was the added excitement—when the students returned to school on Monday—of a short week leading up to Thanksgiving. It had been awhile since wrestle-o-rama at the bowling alley, and John and Jeff had patched up their minor feud. After all, it had only cost them a chance to ever date the Mason cousins again. And the upside was that, when the story spread through school like a brush fire, the two friends achieved a status usually reserved for guys who smoked cigarettes and wore black leather jackets. Seventh graders avoided them in the hallways, and teachers looked down upon them with even more than the usual amount of disdain. No doubt about it. Their legend was growing. But what the boys couldn't possibly guess as they strode into LASS that morning was that the world as they knew it would change forever later that day.

Three times a week, half of third period was set aside for the study of French. Why this was necessary baffled all but the most astute bomars in the school, who claimed it was needed in order for Americans to fit into in an ever-shrinking global society. John, not alone in his belief, could not foresee a time when he would need to ask, "Where is the library?" in French.

Nonetheless, peppy Miss Parras, fluent in four languages, flitted into Mr. Schwartz's room every Monday, Wednesday, and Friday at precisely ten o'clock and chirped, "Bon, bon, bon!" This meant, "Good, good, good," which was most likely an acknowledgment that everyone was in his or her proper seat and no one had lit the room on fire. She followed this with, "Bonjour, messieurs et mesdemoiselles! Comment allez-vous?" to which the class responded in unison, "Très bien, merci. Et vous?"

The twenty-five minutes that followed consisted of one of two lessons. The first: continual instruction in key words and phrases by means of obsessive-compulsive, mind-altering, insanity-producing repetition.

"Quelle heure est-il?"
"Répétez."
"Quelle heure est-il?"
"Répétez."
"Quelle heure est-il?"
"Bon."

The second type of lesson was infinitely harder. Students were paired up to memorize snatches of dialogue, supposedly a lifelike French conversation. John mused that French teens must be dull bunnies if all they ever asked each other about was the weather and what's for Sunday dinner.

After practicing, the pairs were forced to perform the scene in front of the class. For a grade. The obvious dilemma in attempting to short-cut the lesson by learning only one set of lines was that Miss Parras never announced the parts until the students stood, ashen and sweating, in front of their peers. And her sugary smile could turn sour in a second if she suspected that someone was stumbling because the lines hadn't been rehearsed.

"Marie, have you failed to study Madame Banques' part?"

"Oui. Pardonnez-moi, s'il vous plaît." This was said with quivering lips and misty eyes.

Marie (Mary to the common folk) was rudely dismissed, an "F" was recorded, and another poor soul was summoned from the audience to take her place. Shame would forever darken her days.

However, on this day, there was neither practice nor performance. For something had happened in the ever-fluctuating world of popular music. Something that had happened many times before yet was so unique that it really was a "fantastic first." There was a new #1 in town! But it was no Elvis Presley-Ricky Nelson-Bobby Vinton-Shelley Fabares-Leslie Gore-Jan and Dean-Rock 'n' Roll cliché. It was a nun, an honest-to-goodness, livin'-in-a-convent nun. Her not-very-clever-but-certainly-appropriate stage name was The Singing Nun, and the little ditty that was sweeping the nation and would soon top the Billboard Hot 100 chart for an astounding four weeks was titled "Dominique." (Also #1 on Chicago's WLS Silver Dollar Survey.)

Well, one might argue, it *was* the '60s, and, if she could sing, what difference did it make if she dressed in a habit and spent her free time lighting candles? The difference was that, unlike "It's My Party," "Surf City," and "Sugar Shack," the lyrics to "Dominique" were sung in French. This meant that, even without being able to understand a single word, otherwise sane teens were snatching up copies of the 45 as fast as the radio and record shops could stock them. Perhaps they were under the illusion that, if they played it backwards . . .

So, Miss Parras was even more euphoric than usual when she burst into the classroom that day. She was no longer merely a French teacher; she was a French teacher on a mission. In one hand, she lugged a record player by its handle. In her other was a well-worn copy of "Dominique." Wedged under her arm were lyric sheets, the lesson plan for the day. Because, as John's class was soon to find out, Miss Parras was determined to take full advantage of this freak occurrence. She would use the immense popularity of this hit record to infuse her eager pupils with a lifelong love of French.

"Bon, bon, bon! Attention, messieurs et mesdemoiselles!" While passing the handouts around the room, she rambled on. "Today, class, you will all learn the meaning of this beautiful song. And when you hear it on the radio, you can impress your parents by explaining it to them."

John chanced a sideways glance across the room at Jeff, who twirled his right hand in a circle near his ear in the sign for cuckoo.

Miss Parras was now setting up the record player. "The song is a narrative—a story, that is—about a missionary who goes out into the world to tell people about the love of God."

For the love of God, thought John, had Rock 'n' Roll been reduced to this drivel? Was Buddy Holly turning over in his grave?

Apparently so. In front of their faces sat the French and English lyrics, side by side. And it was a stirring story. Miss Parras played the record three times, bouncing jauntily to the catchy tune and encouraging the students to sing along with her. A variety of responses followed, from sweet soprano highs to Bobby Pignatello's belch-along-to-the-music lows.

"Bon, bon, bon! And now, I have a big surprise for all of you! These lyric sheets are yours to keep! So, whenever you hear the song, you can continue to learn what every word or phrase means."

Ah, thought John, hands-on learning. Teachers ate that up. Demented Miss Parras probably pictured students gathered at a sock hop chanting loudly at the student DJ, "We want the nun! Give us the nun!"

John turned to his desk mate Susan Considine, who was loving every minute of the madness. Susan—never Sue or Susie—had sat beside him ever since Mr. Schwartz had moved his buddy Jeff to the other side of the room. A bright, studious overachiever, she was a good influence on John. His study partner for spelling, vocabulary, grammar, and history tests, she pushed him to work hard and even told him once that he was too smart to be hanging around with Jeff and acting like a clown all the time. Inwardly, he knew Susan was right; he'd have to grow up someday.

"You may talk quietly in your seats for the last few minutes before the bell rings," gasped Miss Parras. She was clearly hyperventilating now. "Use your inside voices, s'il vous plaît."

Susan, never one to let an opportunity to acquire more knowledge pass by, began flipping through the pages of her *Weekly Reader*, which had been handed out earlier by Mr. Schwartz.

"I like him," she said to John. She was pointing at a small picture in the magazine.

"Who?" John leaned closer to get a better look.

"President Kennedy. I think he's a smart man. I want to meet him someday."

John's Catholic family admired him too. "When are you ever going to meet the president?"

"I don't know. Maybe next summer. My family and I are going to Washington, D.C., on vacation. My mother told me there are White House tours, and sometimes Mr. and Mrs. Kennedy come out and talk to the visitors."

"Really?" John was only mildly skeptical. Susan usually knew what she was talking about.

"It's true. Anyway, I want to shake his hand and tell him I think he's doing a good job. You know, with civil rights and the Cold War and everything."

"Right," said John, suddenly remembering his crazy Uncle Lou yelling angrily at the TV set last summer, saying that Martin Luther King was as much of a Commie as Khrushchev.

"I just know he'll get re-elected next year. And, by the end of the decade, we'll land a man on the moon, just like he says."

The bell rang. John scooped up his books and headed for gym with a better appreciation of the president. Susan, he thought, deserved to meet him. Who knew? Maybe next summer she would.

***

It had been a weird day, what with The Singing Nun and all. After lunch, John sat in Mr. Weber's science class and tried to pay attention. But it was Friday, and more than once his eyelids felt heavy. He thought about how next week the country would celebrate Thanksgiving. Then, suddenly, the loudspeaker above the door crackled to life. Mr. Reid, the principal, spoke solemnly: "Boys and girls, could I have your undivided attention, please? I have an announcement to make."

This was unheard of. Special announcements were always made either by Mr. Carver or Mrs. Popovic, the all-purpose secretary.

"I hope you will all handle this announcement with propriety and restraint."

What? John and his classmates tensed.

"A short time ago, President Kennedy was shot while riding in a parade in Dallas, Texas. He has been taken to a nearby hospital. When the bell rings in a few minutes, I want you to proceed quietly to your next class. We will place a radio next to our microphone here in the office and allow you to listen to any further news reports. Thank you."

A stunned silence followed. The bell rang, causing more than one student to jump. John and his peers moved zombie-like into the hall. No one spoke; there was nothing to say.

Mr. Schwartz stood sentry-like at the door, nodding gravely to each of his charges as they passed through the entryway. John immediately took his seat and waited. Susan arrived, her face white with fear. She walked as if underwater, head down and shoulders slumped. Sitting, she stared with glazed eyes at the loudspeaker, which now transmitted the fate of a nation.

Little of it made much sense to John. Having been schooled in action-adventure books and TV, he pictured it as a dramatic car chase through the streets with Secret Service agents and would-be assassins exchanging gunfire. The president, sadly, had been wounded. But Mr. Reid had mentioned the hospital. Surely the doctors were taking care of him. Surely he would be okay. Surely he wouldn't . . .

The man on the radio broadcast interrupted John's thoughts: "We have a confirmed report that President Kennedy died at 1:00 Central Standard Time."

Audible gasps and muffled sobs broke out. John looked at Susan. Tears ran down her cheeks as she repeated softly to herself, "That man. That man."

And then John surprised himself. He slid his chair closer and wrapped his arm around Susan's shoulder. She looked into his eyes and tried to thank him with a smile, but it wouldn't come. Then, the uncompromising truth hit her like a truck, and she put her head on his chest and wept.

***

President Lyndon Baines Johnson stood on the tarmac at Andrews Air Force Base, his stoic wife beside him, and spoke into the hastily arranged microphones: "I will do my best. That is all I can do. I ask for your help, and God's."

The weekend trudged by in slow motion. TV stole the show away from the newspapers and Sunday sermons. Jackie's bloodstained dress. The flag-draped casket in the Capitol rotunda. An endless line of citizens standing in the cold rain. Oswald's murder. Monday's majestic military funeral drenched in crisp sunlight. The caisson. The riderless horse. John-John's salute. Images that were burned into the national psyche forever.

John sat stiffly on the couch and watched his father, a rugged laborer and World War II veteran, cry softly. He saw his mother staring at the set with red eyes, emotion having finally given way to numbing shock. He looked back at the TV. They were at the gravesite now. The fly-by with the lead jet absent. The twenty-one gun salute. Jackie reaching out to clutch the folded flag. The lighting of the eternal flame.

Lights were turned off all over America. People climbed into bed, weary from the long weekend. What had been lost could never be regained.

5

It's true that young people bounce back more rapidly from tragedy than adults. And so it was for John and his classmates. Somber November rolled into December, the march toward Christmas gaining momentum every day.

"So, what are you asking your parents to get you for Christmas?" John asked Jeff as they sat across from each other in the crowded cafeteria.

Jeff grinned. "I was thinking about asking for a year's subscription to *Playboy*."

John paused in mid-bite. "Really?"

"No, not really, dipshit. Do you believe everything anyone tells you? Man, you are hopeless."

"Well, I'm asking my folks for an official NFL football."

"Cool. Hey, I almost forgot. Look at this." Jeff dug deep into his pants pocket and pulled out a crumpled envelope. He flung it at John with a smile. "Read it and weep."

John slowly pulled a bright green sheet of paper out of the envelope—Jeff's name was on the front—and unfolded it. The words **"You are invited to a Party!"** leapt out at him.

The invitation was from Gail Swanson, a very popular eighth-grade girl. "**An evening of caroling followed by hot chocolate and snacks!**"

The social was for the upcoming Saturday night, "**7:00 to 10:00 PM**," and directions to Gail's house were provided. John looked up at his still-smiling friend, and envy lunged at him. He tossed the treasure onto the table. "Have a nice time. I've got to be going. Don't wanna be late for old man Weber's class."

John dumped his half-eaten lunch into the nearest trash can and stormed out of the cafeteria. Pushing open the door to the boys' room, he approached the empty set of urinals. As he stood there waiting for the pee to begin flowing, he leaned his head forward against the tile. It was a genuine boy-girl party, John sulked, and he was not invited. He was too much of a loser for someone like Gail and her stuck-up friends to ask. On the other hand, Mr. Suave himself, Jeff Womack, with his shock of black hair and laissez-faire attitude, was most likely first on the list.

John sighed and relaxed. A steady stream of liquid splashed into the basin with an angry urgency.

"Hello there."

John glanced to his right. "What do you want? Are you going to follow me around all day? I already told you to have a nice time at the party. Why don't you just leave me alone?"

"Never, Johnny-me-boy. I love you too much."

John shook himself, zipped up, and stalked to the sink. "Yeah, sure."

As he finished washing his hands, he looked up to see an envelope several inches from his nose—an envelope with "John Belson" written neatly on the front.

"I forgot. Gail Swanson handed me this on the bus this morning and told me to give it to you."

***

John stood close to his bedroom mirror and examined his face for any imperfections. He had last popped a zit three days ago, and none had cropped up since. He reached for the small bottle of Vitalis on his dresser, poured a larger-than-usual amount into his hands, and rubbed it vigorously into his hair. Deftly executing the part to the left of center, he then slid the black comb through the oily mat across the top of his head. Almost satisfied, he patted down his cowlick until it stuck, jammed his comb into his back pocket, and stepped back.

He wore a burgundy button-down shirt with a black dickey. Black trousers and penny loafers over black socks complemented the upper half of the outfit. He looked as cool as any eighth-grade boy could look before he actually interacted with real-live girls in a social setting. At which time sweat would burst forth from his forehead and armpits like Niagara Falls, and stupid sayings would fly from his mouth like locusts.

John slid two shiny pennies into the slots on the vamps of his shoes. Only one item remained on his checklist, but it was the most important one. He picked up the invitation from the top of his dresser—the one he had read a thousand times during the last four days—and stuffed it into his shirt pocket. This was absolutely necessary as there was always the absurd possibility that Gail would forget she had invited him. My God, thought John, swallowing hard. Imagine the humiliation: "Hello, Dad, can you come pick me up? Yeah, I know, but there's been a terrible mix-up."

John's parents dropped him off at Gail's house and watched him walk up the pathway and ring the doorbell. They left only after he shot them a dirty glance or two, suggesting he would be mortified by their mere presence.

A beaming Gail opened the front door. "Hi, John! Welcome to my party! Come on in!"

"Hi," he said, suddenly nervous. But he had no reason to be. Gail had greeted him warmly, and no one had shouted out, "What's *he* doing here?" At least not yet.

John looked past his hostess. Inside was a small gathering of kids—two small gatherings really, girls and boys on separate sides of the fashionably furnished living room. He thought it odd that they were all still wearing coats.

"Leave your coat on for now. As soon as the others arrive, we're going caroling."

Ah, yes. John remembered the invitation's wording.

"Did you bring your boots? There's some snow out there."

Idiot. John knew he'd forgotten something. He shook his head as he looked down at the neat pile of boots that others—the smart ones—had brought along.

"That's okay. You'll be fine. It's not too deep. And, besides, most of the sidewalks are shoveled." Gail was trying her best to be gracious, and John admired her for it.

"Thanks for having me," he said. "I brought along the invitation in case you forgot."

Gail laughed, a genuine reaction. Her teeth sparkled, and her dark hair shone in the entryway light. "Don't worry. I won't kick you out."

John smiled at her and sidled over to his own kind. Jeff wasn't there yet, but his old Little League friend Bill Dobbs, Miller Junior High's self-described "make-out king," was.

"Hey, John, what're you doing here?"

"I received an invitation, just like you."

"Fat chance. You probably stole one."

"So, how've you been? I haven't seen you around much."

It was true. In typical junior high fashion, friendships were forged and broken by schedules more than anything else. And, save for lunch and locker time, John and Bill seldom crossed paths during the day.

"Couldn't be better. You see Lynn Folsom over there? We're going out. Took her to see *From Russia With Love* last weekend. Funny thing, I can't recall the plot."

"I can't believe your parents let you see a James Bond movie." Every Sunday morning after Mass, John's mom would snatch up the little movie guide from the rack in the vestibule. Prepared by the ultraconservative Catholic Church, it rated movies for their family appropriateness. Disney films like *Swiss Family Robinson* and *Pollyanna* always received "A" grades; a spy thriller with random killings and casual sex received a "C," the ultimate kiss of death.

"They dropped Lynn and me at the bowling alley. We walked to the theatre and back again. Hey, what Mom and Pop don't know can't hurt them, right?"

"I guess."

Bill draped his large arm over John's shoulder. "Listen to me. Life's short. I mean, look at Kennedy. One minute you're alive, and the next . . ."

John pulled away. "Don't talk about him like that."

"Look, all I'm saying is you've gotta start having some fun. We'll be in high school next year, and the girls will be like so many stars in the sky."

John rolled his eyes at the bad poetry.

"A little bird told me there's gonna be some dancing tonight after the stupid caroling. The girls have been collecting 45s all week. So, who do you like?"

"I'm not sure," said John, giving himself away by shifting his eyes toward the front door, where Gail was still standing. He had spent the last few nights lying awake in bed thinking about why she had asked him to her party. Maybe she liked him.

"Oh, I see you have a taste for the delectable Miss Swanson. Good choice. Now, when the dancing begins, make your move before somebody else does. I guarantee you she'll love it if you ask her to dance. It's how we operate here in the civilized world."

Jeff's sudden appearance silenced Bill's well-meant but condescending advice. "Hello, gentlemen. Ready to sing for your supper?"

Sandwiched between two prima donnas, John began to reconsidered his decision to attend the party.

"Attention, everybody!" Gail's voice cut through the chatter. "We're going out now, so bundle up. And don't forget to grab the sheet music as you leave. It's on the table by the front door."

Sheet music? What was that all about? mused John. Every kid in his generation knew the words to all the Christmas carols and seasonal songs. And then he remembered—Mrs. Roman. Two weeks ago, John's class had left the devil-may-care madness of art and moved to music, the second of their three required "extras."

Mrs. Roman, John had learned, was as passionate about music as Mr. Robinson was about art. In fact, at eight o'clock in the morning, she was a bit over-the-top. With her ridiculous hairstyle—long and straight and parted down the middle, one side colored black and the other white—she reminded John immediately of Cruella De Vil. Her personality fit the bill as well.

She would pound the piano and wail out song after song, stopping only to screech at her students when they were off-key: "Backs straight! No slouching! Breathe in and out! Feel the music within you! It's alive!"

John wondered at times if she, like Frankenstein's Monster, was "alive." And was she, too, made up of spare body parts? Her zombie-like face—bright red lipstick and blue eye shadow on a palette of white—suggested she had once been dead. And she was new to the school that very year. Where *had* she come from?

John was snapped back to reality as the partygoers surged forward.

Reaching the table, he obediently picked up a stapled packet of sheet music. Mrs. Roman's indoctrination had taken hold, at least with the girls. John and his scruffy male comrades would just as soon have sung Big Ten fight songs from memory.

***

An hour later, a cold, wet, tired, hungry herd of teens pushed their way back into Gail Swanson's heated home. Boots, coats, gloves, scarves, and hats were dumped in a bundle, and the half-frozen figures clamored down the basement steps to the finished rec room below. Gail's parents were there to pass out hot chocolate and Jingles, the anise-flavored Christmas cookies shaped like stars, bells, wreaths, and trees. John was somewhat surprised. Although delicious, these treats were store-bought. He had pictured Gail and her mother slaving over homemade cookies smothered in colored frosting and decorated with nonpareils. Well, goodies were goodies, and John was starving. He was damp to the bone too, but the hot chocolate would cure that.

"Aaaaah!" John spat the burning liquid back into the cup, the resultant splash landing squarely on his hand and wrist. He looked up to see Jeff smiling in his direction, casually blowing across the lip of his own steaming drink.

"Hot, huh?"

Yeah, thought John, certain he would never again feel the roof of his mouth.

"So, who're you planning on asking to dance?"

At this point, John didn't care. His face was frozen, his hand was scalded, his tongue was swollen, and his socks were soaked. Truth be told, he just wanted to go home, crawl into a warm bed, and admit defeat.

"If everybody had an ocean . . ." The Beach Boys blared from the record player, and a buzz swarmed through the crowd. Squeals of delight shook off the doldrums of winter as the teens paired off, suddenly transported to the shores of the Pacific.

"Would you like to dance?"

John looked up from his misery into the encouraging eyes of Gail Swanson. Was this a vision? Had the hot chocolate burned its way into his brain?

And then an amazing thing happened, one that John would remember for the rest of his life. Gail reached out, took the cup of cocoa from his hand, and set it down on the nearby Ping-Pong table. Then, she grabbed his uninjured hand and pulled him out onto the dance floor.

And John danced. Not only with Gail, but with other girls as well. It was as if his wretched, lonely, friendless seventh-grade year had never taken place. And somehow, bobbing and weaving and twisting and shaking, he felt like himself again.

6

John Belson and Jeff Womack had been reasonably well behaved of late. What with Mr. Carver's phone calls home and the coming of Christmas, the boys figured it was a good time to cut back on the shenanigans. Sitting beside each other in their first-period music class just waiting for Mrs. Roman to arrive like something out of Mussorgsky's "Night on Bald Mountain," they basked in their ever-increasing popularity.

"You were a wild man on the dance floor at Swanson's the other night," observed Jeff. "I didn't know you had it in you."

John smiled. "It was fun." In truth, he hadn't had so much carefree, energetic fun in almost two years. And it felt good to be accepted again. No one had taunted him about his weight or his glasses or anything.

"Hey, guys. What's up?" The high-pitched voice belonged to the diminutive Petey O'Neal. But his strength belied his small stature. Wiry and tough, he was a standout on the school's wrestling team. John thought him to be the most annoying boy he'd ever met, and his overt friendliness signaled only the arrival of trouble.

"Nothing's up, Petey," said a wary Jeff.

"So," he continued, shifting his eyes to cast an amused gaze down upon John, "I heard you danced with Gail Swanson at her party the other night."

Suddenly, it was as if Jeff wasn't even there. Petey, smirking, bore down on John. "Funny. I was talking to Gail and some of her friends just a few minutes ago by their lockers. And they all said the same thing. You know what that was?"

A deathly silence pervaded the room, the calm before the storm. John felt stares directed at him. He guessed what was coming, but it was like he was trapped in a coffin, unable to move or speak. Where the hell was Mrs. Roman?

"They said you didn't know how to dance!" The derisive words and ensuing laughter delivered a crushing blow to John's soul. Pain shot through him like a scorpion's sting, freezing his body. But only for a second.

Before Jeff could stop him, John flung himself out of his chair and tackled Petey. The combined weight of their bodies crashed into several music stands, sending Mrs. Roman's beloved sheet music sailing into space.

The element of surprise was huge. John clenched Petey's collar with both hands, lifted his head off the floor, and banged it down again, hard. Petey winced.

"Shut up! You hear me? Shut up!"

In the next moment, John's body was being forcibly lifted off the smaller boy, pulled up from behind by Jeff.

"Let me go!"

"Cut it out! That's enough!"

Petey rolled away and shot to his feet. He stood with eyes opened wide, scarcely believing what had just happened. The back of his head hurt, but he restrained from rubbing it. Instead, he spat on the floor and scowled at John. "This isn't over, Belson."

"Yes, it is," said Jeff, his arms locked around John's waist. "Take a hike, or I'll pound you myself."

A hint of fear crept into Petey's eyes, and he withdrew with as much dignity as possible to the other side of the room.

John shook off Jeff and turned to face him. "I don't need you to fight my battles for me."

"Like hell. He wasn't just going to let you beat him into the ground, you know. Besides, if any punches were thrown, you'd both be in Carver's office. You were lucky Cruella wasn't here yet. Now, help me pick up this stuff before she comes in."

Mrs. Roman burst into the room moments later. "Sorry I'm late, boys and girls! I was out in the hall having a conversation with Mr. Donovan."

Ah, the good old days, thought John. Mr. Donovan had taught music to last year's seventh graders, one of the only bright spots in the entire year. Mr. "D," as the kids called him, had encouraged them to sing "Puff the Magic Dragon" for the fun of it, and he didn't care if a non-musical type copied his report on Mozart from the *World Book Encyclopedia* as long as the margins were straight.

Mrs. Roman continued, "I do want to compliment you, however, on your outstanding behavior. We were right outside the door and never heard a peep."

The class snickered.

Jeff whispered to John, "God, she must be deaf. No wonder she sings like she does."

For the rest of the period, John massaged his elbow, swollen from where it had struck the tile beneath Petey's body, and reflected on what had transpired. A year ago, he would have just sat there like a lump and let the bully shred his spirit. This time, he had fought back. And although he was thankful for Jeff's intervention, he wasn't ashamed of his actions.

Painful possibilities gnawed at John's psyche, however. Petey was an ass-clown, and nothing short of a lobotomy would ever cure that. But it was doubtful that he would make up these statements. Had Gail, who had been so kind to John at her party, really said that he didn't know how to dance? Had she and her friends stood around giggling at his efforts merely to amuse one another on a Monday morning?

John's head sank as an awful truth hit him. He had only been invited to the party in the first place because he was Jeff's friend. The girls had been afraid that the tall, handsome cowboy wouldn't come unless they also asked his fat, dopey sidekick. That's why Gail had given Jeff both invitations; she couldn't, in good conscience, hand one to John in person. And now, only two days after the girls had made him feel reborn, they were laughing at him behind his back.

But, as it turned out, this was not the case at all. John's confidence soared once more when, the day after the dustup, Gail Swanson herself approached him at his locker to tell him that she'd heard Petey was making up stuff about her and not to believe the lies. She added that she was glad John had decked him.

"Making up stuff," she said, and John realized he had been wanted and accepted at the party. It was Petey, who had very intentionally *not* been invited to the party, who was jealously inventing rumors to make himself look better.

But, in spite of his threat, the resentful boy kept his distance during the two weeks leading up to Christmas vacation. John surmised that he was afraid of what Jeff might do to him; but, more than anything, he hoped Petey remembered that John could—and would—stand up for himself.

So, as he banged his locker shut on the Friday afternoon before Christmas, John Belson smiled. He was no longer the lonely boy he had been the day school started. He had a best friend, guys didn't pick on him, and girls were beginning to like him again. He had come a long way in four short months.

"Hey, John." Jeff caught him from behind as he headed down the stairs. "Gimme a call after Christmas. We'll do something together."

"Okay."

The two boys burst through the doorway into the cold sunlight, split up, and climbed onto their separate buses.

7

John waited until the Saturday after Christmas before he dialed Jeff's house. He knew Jeff would be away visiting relatives in Wisconsin until then.

"Hello." It was Jeff's mom.

"Hello, Mrs. Womack. This is John Belson. Is Jeff there?"

"Just one minute. Jeff! Phone! It's John!"

"Hello, sugar lips. It's been awhile."

John laughed. Post-Christmas boredom had tightened its hold on him, and it picked him up just to hear Jeff's voice. "So, how was Wisconsin?"

"Mostly white."

"No, I mean how was Christmas? Did you get anything cool?"

"As a matter of fact, I did." Jeff's parents had given him a Sylvania transistor radio. "Did you get your NFL football?"

"Yep. That's why I was calling you. You wanna get together and watch the Bears tomorrow? It's the Championship game, you know."

"How could I not know? I just spent a week in Packer country, remember? My Uncle Barney was shittin' bricks over it. He kept ranting about how, if Paul Hornung hadn't been suspended this year, the Pack would have won it all again."

But they wouldn't get the chance. They had lost the Western Division, finishing 11-2-1 to the Bears' 11-1-2, their only two losses courtesy of the Monsters of the Midway. Without their "Golden Boy"—Hornung and Detroit's Alex Karras had sat out the entire season as a punishment for gambling on games—not even Vince Lombardi could guide Green Bay to its third straight NFL title.

So, it was the Bears then, coached by the legendary George Halas, who would face off against the New York Giants in Chicago's Wrigley Field on Sunday, Dec. 29th.

"Your place or mine?" Jeff asked suggestively.

John laughed again. "We're gonna have to go to St. James. It's blacked out."

"What? The Championship game isn't on TV?"

"Not in Chicago."

In spite of the fact that Wrigley Field would be stuffed to the rafters with frostbitten fans, the most sacred of all NFL rules prevailed over common sense: only *road* games, in black-and-white, were beamed locally throughout the entire season.

"Oh, crap. We have to pay to watch it?"

"Fifty cents."

"Fifty cents? That's a rip-off."

"Where else you gonna watch it?"

John was right. There was no place else. The church, simply by turning its massive aerial atop its adjoining school toward Rockford, could pick up a snowy TV picture. As heads of a non-profit organization, the priests were given dispensation by the local authorities, allowing them to charge parishioners to view Bears home games every year. A medium-sized television was set up facing rows of metal chairs in the school's basement. Because the school's heat was turned way down on weekends, the frigid air gave the fans the feeling they were actually at the games, an inspired dose of realism. Dads brought their sons and bonded with fellow Catholics in the sterile environment. No food or drink was allowed, not even candy. And if anyone swore, he was immediately evicted—no money back—by Father Costello, who supervised these matinees.

***

On Sunday afternoon, bundled against the elements, John trudged through the fresh snow to St. James, where Jeff, coming from the opposite direction, was to meet him. During Mass that morning, the faithful had been reminded of the sweet deal during Father Lawrence's homily.

". . . and just as David slew the mighty Goliath, so will the Bears rise up and slay the Giants this afternoon, God willing. And remember, although this epic contest of strength and stamina will be blacked out in the Chicago area, it can be seen in its entirety in the school's basement for a small donation of only fifty cents per person. All are welcome."

And all came. By the time John, weary from his walk, entered the large, undecorated room, it looked like an SRO crowd. Packed with excited fans, the metal chairs began only a few feet from the television, which was placed atop an old wardrobe, and stretched out to the back wall fifty yards away.

"Hello, John. Nice to see you here," beamed Father Costello, his puffy hands holding out a large basket full of money.

"Hello, Father," said John, removing his hat and tugging his scarf away from his frozen face.

"It's fifty cents to stay."

"I know." John reached into the pocket of his corduroys, pulled out two quarters, and placed them in the basket. He turned and looked out over the buzzing crowd; the game had begun.

"Father, have you seen Jeff Womack? He was supposed to meet me here."

"That's the new boy, isn't it? The tall, dark-haired boy?"

"Yes, sir."

Father Costello cast a disapproving look down upon John. "You know, you might consider choosing your friends more carefully. He doesn't seem to me to be the type of boy you should be hanging around with. He has a troubled past. Remember, John, always avoid the near temptation of sin."

"Yes, Father."

The door crashed open. "Sorry I'm late."

The delirious crowd halted in mid-cheer to stare at the noisy newcomer.

"Can't you ever come in quietly?" hissed an embarrassed John.

"Jeff Womack, isn't it?" said Father Costello, his lips pressed into a tight frown.

"Yes, Father."

"That'll be fifty cents to stay."

Jeff looked stunned. "You mean it costs to watch the game?"

John cast his eyes to the floor. What was Jeff up to?

"I'm sorry, sir. I don't have any money on me."

"Didn't you listen to Father Lawrence at Mass this morning? He mentioned the donation. It's for the Sisters of the Poor."

"Yes, sir, and like he said, it's a donation. So, if it's a donation, then it isn't required. Isn't that right, Father?"

Father Costello's face went red. He glanced over at John, who was still staring at his boots. "John, perhaps you have some more change to loan your friend. Do you?"

"I don't, Father."

For a second, Father Costello weighed his options. The basket, heavy in his hands, told him a killing had already been made. And although he obviously didn't have much compassion for the new boy, he couldn't make a scene in front of his flock, which was waiting to witness the outcome.

"Very well," he smiled, the blood draining from his face. "You may stay. I believe there are still a couple of seats in the back row."

Charity had won the day. The group of men and boys shifted its focus back to the screen.

John and Jeff squeezed into the last row and sat down on the cold chairs. They could barely see the TV.

"Fifty cents, my ass," said Jeff. "These are the nickel seats."

John's patience broke. "What are you complaining for? You didn't pay, remember?" Before Jeff could come back with a wisecrack, John poured it on. "What's the matter with you, anyway? You knew you were supposed to bring money with you. I told you that. So, what is this? Another 'I'll show them' exhibit? Does it excite you to constantly annoy people in authority? Do you need the attention that badly? Shame on you, stealing money from the church."

"Now, wait a minute . . ."

"No, you wait. It's one thing to screw around at school. But this is different. I asked you to come with me today because you're my friend, and we have fun together. But, so help me, if I'd known you were going to willfully cheat Father Costello, I would have come here by myself."

Jeff crossed his arms and sank sullenly down in his seat. For once, he had no clever retort. John's accusation had hit home, and both boys knew it.

Sitting in silence, they stared ahead in the general direction of the TV. John felt bad that he had launched a full frontal attack on his best friend. After all, if it hadn't been for Jeff, he would still be on his own. No parties. No dances. No girls. No self-confidence. And no one made him laugh like Jeff did, often at the most inane things. What did he care that Father Costello got gypped out of a lousy fifty cents? Wasn't their bond worth a whole lot more than that? And yet . . .

"I'm sorry. You're right." It was Jeff who spoke. "I didn't mean to ruin everything. I just thought it would be funny to mess with Father Costello, you know, to see what he'd do. I guess it was a jerky thing to do."

John didn't answer right away. He wasn't sure what to say. He admired Jeff, and he felt awkward that his friend had suddenly apologized to him. "Forget it. Let's watch the game."

And as John watched the Bears take down the Giants, a different kind of thought pushed its way into his head. Maybe Jeff—handsome, boisterous—needed someone like John to keep him on steady ground. Maybe it wasn't so easy to be the new kid who was always saying or doing something outrageous so everyone would notice him. Perhaps, in an unspoken, frightening way, Jeff Womack was lonely too.

8

The aftermath of Christmas vacation always hit hard. This was especially true in the Midwest, where colored lights and toy displays were replaced with snow, ice, wind, and bitter cold. Naked Christmas trees, abandoned atop soiled mounds of street snow, sat like death-row inmates awaiting the arrival of the garbage truck.

The first day back at school, a field trip to an all-too-familiar Hell. Had there ever been two weeks of Heaven? First period with Mrs. Roman was a chamber of horrors, from her new beehive hairdo to the strident sound of her voice: "Come alive! Make sweet music for me!" Mr. Schwartz seemed tired as he exhorted his charges to prepare for the last lap of junior high. Apparently, there was still much grammar and history to learn. Miss Parras, not as smug since The Singing Nun had been blessedly bumped from the top of the charts, paired students off to begin memorizing a sorry scene in which some stupid kid couldn't find the library in his own school: "Où est la bibliothèque?" In gym, Mr. Dumpmore, assuming that all broken blood vessels and swollen bruises had healed, lined up teams for yet another rousing dodge ball battle. He just never tired of hearing those screams.

By the time lunch rolled around, John and Jeff were physically and emotionally exhausted.

"My Lord, what a long day!" John stared at his chicken sandwich and tater tots, too tired to be hungry.

"I'm not sure I can survive the next five months." Jeff had a point. The beginning of June, when they would hopefully graduate, seemed a million miles away. And there was more bad news waiting to greet them after lunch.

From now on, they would be given only twenty-five minutes to eat. Mr. Carver had come to the conclusion that there was too much time for students to finish their lunches quickly and then cause trouble in the cafeteria. Right before Christmas vacation, there had been a food fight, resulting in a boy-girl seating chart. For one week, the eighth grade, pressed in by members of the opposite sex, ate in subdued silence. The girls were especially grossed out by the boys' eating habits.

But that was only a temporary fix. Mr. Carver, in a brief moment of brilliance, decided to shorten lunch and then herd the students into the girls' gym for the last twenty minutes. There, boys and girls, segregated across the polished wooden floor from one another, would sit and talk quietly until the bell rang.

But, unfortunately, that was not all. Upon hearing of the plan, the student council convinced Mr. Carver to allow dancing. A record player was set up at one end of the long room, scratchy 45s were donated, and the duly elected officials proceeded with their power play.

In all fairness, John had to admit, the idea took off with wings. By the end of the first week back, more and more boys were putting their lives on the line by making the brisk walk across the floor to ask a girl to dance. One was sent back, head hung in humiliation, jeered at by friends. Another took advantage of the slow, romantic songs of the day—"Hey Paula," "Blue Velvet," "Go Away Little Girl"—by sliding a hand around an angel's waist and gently pulling her closer to him. One girl, enchanted by the magic of it all, dropped her head onto the boy's shoulder. A familiar greaser-slut couple pressed their bodies together and made out, not at all aware of envious onlookers.

Jeff, never playing favorites, danced several times with different girls that first week. John, frightened by the very real prospect of rejection, held back. It was true; he had come a long way. But dancing in front of the entire eighth grade was for people like Bill Dobbs, who clung lecherously to Lynn Folsom, not for people like him. That was until he saw *her* for the first time.

It was Friday. The long week was almost over; the weekend perched like a songbird in the near distance. John and

Jeff plopped down next to each other on the hardwood floor. They watched a group of girls, giggling about nothing, file past them. Following them was a pretty girl who walked alone. John's first impression of her was that, although she carried herself in a dignified manner, she did not choose to be so isolated. She appeared to be friendless. This was confirmed when, her shimmering black hair falling casually across her shoulders, she sat down by herself in a far corner and pulled a paperback from her purse.

"You want to know who she is?" Jeff's voice broke into John's trance.

"Do you know?"

"Never seen her before. But I can find out. I'll ask some of the girls in Mrs. Danforth's homeroom. They'll know." Jeff smiled. "Don't worry. I won't blab it all over that you're smitten."

"I'm not smitten," John lied. "Just curious."

"Whatever you say. Anyway, you can trust me. And now, if you don't mind, I'm going to ask Lori Tortello to dance."

John spent the next fifteen minutes staring across the gym. She sat, saddle shoes tucked beneath a plaid skirt and head down, engrossed in whatever she was reading. Once or twice, she looked up. Even at this distance, her unadorned beauty stood out. Her milky face, framed by her raven hair and a navy blue turtleneck, appeared almost spirit-like to John. Her eyes—what color were they?—darted about as if searching for someone. She saw no one she recognized and returned to her book. Was it possible, John thought, that she had been in school since September and he had never laid eyes on her? No. Impossible. She must be new. But where did she come from? What was her name?

***

"Michelle. Nobody seems to know her last name. She moved here from out East somewhere, Ohio maybe, or Pennsylvania. When she introduced herself to Mrs. Danforth's class, she said she lived with her mother. She didn't say where her father was, or if she even had one." Jeff paused to let the brief biography sink in. "Are you going to ask her out, or at least to dance?"

"Michelle." John spoke her name softly, numbed by the thought of knowing even this little about her. He desperately wanted to know more. "Michelle."

"We've covered that. I asked if you're going to—"

"I heard you the first time. I don't know yet. I suppose. Maybe."

"Scared?"

"Yes. I don't think she'll dance with me."

"And what if she doesn't?"

"It's a long walk back."

"True."

"Maybe I should try to talk to her first. Do you know where her locker is?"

"Well, she's new. So, whatever her last name is, they probably stuck her down near the end."

"Near you?"

"Precisely."

John considered the validity of the deduction. Yes, she would be out of alphabetical order, assigned to a locker after the "Zs." "Well, have you seen her down at your end?"

"Haven't looked."

John sighed in exasperation. "Look, could you help me out here?"

"I have a better idea. After school today, why don't you mosey on down and visit me? Then you can check it out for yourself."

"I'll miss my bus."

Jeff flared up. "Speaking of buses, are you gonna go through life like a man waiting for one? Have you ever considered how pathetic that is? You know what your problem is? You never take chances."

John hesitated, stunned by the veracity of Jeff's accusation. "I suppose my mom could pick me up."

"That's more like it. Tell her you stayed after to get extra help in math. Parents love it when you tell 'em that."

"Okay, but make sure you're there as soon as possible so I don't look like I'm wandering around lost or something."

"Yes, boss."

***

Mr. Carver had recently lifted the ban on John and Jeff, allowing them to once again participate in ninth-period electives. The only caveat was that they were not to choose the same one. This was fine with both John, who had longed for chess club, and Jeff, who preferred an activity called "winter sports."

"Check—and mate."

As was required, John reached across the chessboard and shook hands with the winner. "Good game." He glanced at his watch for the umpteenth time. Five minutes to go. He had not been paying attention the entire match, leaving his queen unprotected early in the contest. It had been all downhill from there. But he really didn't care. Sweat beads popped out on his forehead, and his stomach cramped up.

When the bell finally rang, he lunged out the door and ran recklessly down the hall toward Jeff's locker. Arriving moments later, he clutched his friend's arm. "Is she here yet?"

"I haven't seen her. Relax. Act casual."

John wiped his sleeve across his brow and leaned against a locker. The stakeout was on.

"Here she comes."

John's neck shot to the left.

She moved easily, eyes forward, weaving in and out among the raucous crowd. As she walked by, she seemed forlorn, as if the happy madness surrounding her was something she could not relate to. She stopped at the last locker. There, books cradled under her left arm, she slowly spun her combination lock.

"Well, chess master, it's your move."

John swallowed hard. His throat was dry. "What should I say to her?"

"Be natural. Introduce yourself. Tell her you noticed her during lunch, and ask her if maybe she would like to dance sometime. Go ahead, lover boy."

The scream froze the boys—and everyone else. John looked over to see her standing with her hands pressed against her cheeks, her body shaking spasmodically. Her books were scattered at her feet. Instinctively, John walked rapidly toward her. Jeff was close behind.

She met them with tears in her eyes, not the way John had envisioned their first conversation.

"What's wrong?"

She pointed.

On the floor of her locker was a snake. It gave John a momentary start, but he quickly realized it was inanimate—a black rubber reptile. He looked back down the crowded hallway to see Petey O'Neal surrounded by several attractive girls, laughing among themselves.

John reached into the viper's pit. "Don't worry. It's a fake."

The knowledge that it was not real helped little, and she crumpled to the floor like a shattered vase of spring flowers.

Handing off the offensive object to Jeff, John knelt beside the broken beauty. "It's okay. It was just somebody's idea of a joke."

She wept.

Confusion swept through John's mind like a random tornado. He felt sorrow—at this sweet soul's breakdown. He felt anger—at Petey and the girls. And he felt guilt—hadn't he and Jeff howled at Margie Bruce's reaction to their sick practical joke earlier in the year? But mostly, he felt helpless. He didn't know quite what to do or say.

"I gotta go," said Jeff. "I'll miss my bus."

John shot him a dirty look.

"Good luck."

The hallway gradually emptied. Before long, she stopped sobbing. In gentlemanly fashion, John reached into his shirt pocket and handed her a clean handkerchief. She dabbed at her puffy eyes.

"Thank you," she said, and John would only later remember that these were the first words she ever spoke to him.

His knee sore from the hard tile, John sank into a sitting position beside her. "They're jerks, you know." He gestured to the abandoned hallway.

"I know," she said matter-of-factly, as if resigned to her fate as a newcomer.

"Everybody here's not like that." As he said it, a mocking pig's head flashed before his eyes.

She smiled warmly at him. It was the prettiest smile John had ever seen. Their eyes locked. Ah, brown, noticed John.

"I'm Michelle. Michelle Watson. I'm new."

"Yeah, I figured. I'm John Belson. I'm old."

Michelle laughed.

"May I help you up?"

"I think I can manage."

They both scrambled to their feet. John reached down and began to pick up her books. Michelle leaned down to help.

"Oh, no, John. You've missed your bus, haven't you?"

"Yeah, I'll have to call my mom. But what about you?"

"I only live two blocks away. I walk back and forth every day."

John smiled. He didn't know what to say next.

Michelle lifted her coat from the locker and slipped it on. When John handed her books to her, their hands touched. The universe shifted.

"Thanks again. I'm sorry I caused such a commotion. I guess I was having a bad day."

John was sure he was having the most fantastic day of his life. "It's okay. Glad I could help."

"Will I see you tomorrow?"

Tomorrow, mused John, and every day for eternity. "Sure."

"Bye, then." And she was down the stairs and out a side door before John, dumbstruck, could respond.

The lovesick boy had trouble speaking for the rest of the day.

9

John Belson was confused. During the two weeks since he had saved Michelle from the rubber snake, she did not seem overly excited to see him. Because she walked to school, she almost always arrived at her locker, gathered her books, and headed off to her first-period class before John's bus dropped him off. Whenever he tried to talk to her—usually after school—she was always polite but curt, cutting off any attempt by John to make in-depth conversation. At lunch, she sat at the end of a long table of girls, who treated her as they would an empty chair. In the gym, she took her familiar spot in the far corner and read, only occasionally looking up and never, John noted with ever-deepening despair, in his direction. Goaded by Jeff to ask her to dance, his innate shyness took over, refusing to allow him to do so. Apparently, a stalemate of sorts had developed.

Her frequent absences bothered John more than anything else. Was she sick with some weird disease that was slowly taking her life? Or did she just hate school and the sadness of being surrounded by souls but having no one with whom to connect?

"Earth to John. Earth to John. Prepare for splashdown." Jeff's voice cut through John's constipated brain matter.

"What is it?"

"Wow, you're there. I thought you were lost in space. Glad to see you made it home alive, Mr. Glenn."

Annoyed, John sighed loudly.

The boys sat together in music class. They were free to talk in whispers while Mrs. Roman called individual students up to the piano to try out for mixed choir.

"Do-re-me-fa-so-la-te-do!"

"Beautiful, beautiful, Miss Hecht! You simply must fill out our soprano section!"

Janey Hecht would have little choice in the matter. If Mrs. Roman thought a student's voice was good enough, an official letter was sent home to the parents, requesting permission for their child to join. It was a given that, exploding with pride, they would gladly grant it, thus forcing their offspring to attend the ninth-period rehearsals in anticipation of a gala evening concert in early March. It was the last thing in the world that John and Jeff expected to happen to them, like being blindsided by an ice ball.

"So, what have you been brooding about? Could it be that a certain young lady doesn't want to be seen in public with you?"

"Shut up," John hissed.

"I thought so."

"Mr. Womack! It's your turn!"

Jeff slid out of his chair, winked at John, and said, "Move over, Elvis. Here comes the choir's new soloist."

John immediately returned to thinking about Michelle. The truth was he thought about her day and night. In LASS, trying to pay attention to Mr. Schwartz's attempts to drill Civil War history into his students; at his bedroom desk, trying to concentrate on his math homework; in bed, trying to drift off to sleep. All in vain.

"What? You're kidding!" Jeff's voice echoed from the front of the large room. "Are you sure that's a good idea?"

"Oh, yes, Mr. Womack. You have a lovely voice. It reminds me of Andy Williams singing 'Moon River.'"

As the crestfallen boy dragged himself to the back row, he was met by John's smile, the first he had seen in awhile.

"Say nothing and live."

John said nothing. It was just as well. Less than five minutes later, he was also on board the Titanic. In spite of his protests—"But I sing like a dog!" and "I'll miss chess club!"—John was drafted into Mrs. Roman's army.

But later that day, as John pouted his way through Miss Parras' French lesson, Mrs. Roman threw him a sizable bone.

She chose for her beloved choir a quiet, dark-haired girl who was new in school and who—given the chance—sang like an angel.

***

". . . and Michelle Watson will have the other solo, for 'Ave Maria.'" The last week of January had seen Mrs. Roman assign parts to her newly appointed choir. Now, a month of strenuous rehearsals would follow in preparation for the upcoming concert.

John had originally been upset that he hadn't been allowed to say "no" to choir and stay in chess club. But that attitude had, of course, changed overnight upon crawling dejectedly into the first meeting and seeing Michelle, like sweet sugar, sitting in the front row.

John saw this as nothing less than divine intervention. An opportunity was being placed before him, and he had to force himself to rise up and grasp it. The planets aligned on Friday when Mrs. Roman asked Michelle to stay after school to work on her solo. John's heart leapt with joy.

"Aren't you coming?" asked Jeff as students, eager to begin the weekend, poured out of the choir room.

"No. I'm going to use the phone in the lobby to call home and tell my mom I'm staying after."

"What for?"

"So I can talk to Michelle."

"Risky move. I like it. Good luck."

Self-doubt swept over John as he scurried to the school's only pay phone. He inserted a dime and dialed the familiar number.

"Hello, Mom? I gotta stay after. No, I'm not being punished. I need math help again." John wondered if his mom thought he was the slowest student in school. "Pick me up at 4:30, okay? Thanks. Bye."

The anxious boy slammed the receiver back into place and raced through the now deserted hallways back to the choir room. Stopping short of the big double door, he tiptoed the last few feet until he could peer surreptitiously through the glass windows.

Mrs. Roman, perched on the piano bench, had her back to him. To the side, in profile, stood Michelle. She was not singing but rather soaking up instructions on how to approach the difficult song. She smiled and nodded at the teacher.

John, standing slightly away from the glass, was quite certain that, although he could see Michelle clearly, she could not see him. The low winter's sunlight cast its radiant beams through the high windows and onto her face, framing it in fiery glow. If she appeared angelic to John, the imagery was completed when she opened her mouth to sing. Then, as from Heaven's realm, came the soft strains of the most beautiful voice he had ever heard.

The voice was louder now, building to a crescendo. The very core of John's being was climbing higher and higher with it. His body swayed slowly in time with the song. For a brief moment, his eyes clouded over, and he felt as if he might faint.

"Hey, Belson." The voice, like fingernails on a chalkboard, startled John out of his dreamlike state.

He swiveled his head to meet the sardonic smile of Petey O'Neal.

"Whatcha doin', moron? Practicing your dance moves?"

John swallowed hard. He took a step backward and clenched his fists, remembering Petey's prediction that their conflict wasn't settled.

"Relax, fat ass. I'm just comin' out of detention, and I don't wanna go back. I'll pound you some other time."

"What d'ya want, Petey?"

"Nothin'. I just wanted to see what you were starin' at, that's all." Petey turned his face toward the double door's windows. "Ha," he barked derisively. "I thought so. Are you here to protect her from more snakes? You were quite the shining knight that day, saving her and all. Did she reward you with a little tongue?"

"Look, I'm just waiting to talk to Mrs. Roman," John stammered, the flush of embarrassment on his face contradicting the lie.

"Sure you are. And I'm here to try out for your fag-boys choir."

John thought Petey must be deranged. What other reason for his hatred of so many of his peers?

Petey shrugged and smiled again. "Look, it's okay with me if you wanna go after her. She's not my type."

John was growing weary of the one-sided conversation. But he resolved not to allow Petey to provoke him into fighting a second time. Yet John sensed with rising discomfort that his adversary wasn't finished yet; something was coming. What was it? What did Petey know? A vague fear clutched at John's throat.

Suddenly, Petey turned and walked down the hall a short distance, as if securing some space between them before his revelation. Then, he spun around to face John. He wet his lips and spoke. "Now, don't throw a tantrum again, Belson, but I thought you should know. Her mother's a fall-down drunk."

John blanched.

"Ever wonder why she's absent so much? She has to take care of her mommy 'cause her daddy ran off."

John's head hurt, Petey's relentless verbal blows finding their mark.

"Hey, I've got an idea. Why don't you walk her home today and help her clean up the puke?"

Petey had been slowly retreating during his diatribe. With a sudden burst of speed, he was halfway up the staircase, his laughter reverberating behind him.

John, shaken and dizzy, leaned into the wall and shut his eyes. Behind him, he could hear Michelle's voice filtering out through the doorway. What to think? Had the school's biggest liar been telling the truth? What did it mean?

It meant, John realized, that Michelle was an itinerant outcast with no father and an alcoholic mother. No wonder she hadn't allowed John to get close to her. She couldn't bear for him to find out.

Tears pressed themselves out of the corners of John's eyes, and he reached his hand up and wiped them away. He punched his fist hard—two times—against the unforgiving slab of cement, imagining it to be Petey's grimacing, butt-ugly face. If only the jerk had kept his big mouth shut. If only Michelle had a normal life. If only John's world had remained unstained, an angel's voice serenading him in song. But what happened next was no one's fault but his own.

John resolutely pulled himself from the wall, glanced through the glass at Michelle, and walked with head held high away from his pain. It was a coward's path.

10

"Ladies and gentlemen, the Beatles!"

John stared in amazement at the black-and-white image flickering across the television screen. His parents were at a Sunday evening meeting at St. James to organize a fundraiser for the parish's new addition. He wouldn't have normally watched "The Ed Sullivan Show," but Gail Swanson had shown him some fan magazine loaded with pictures of the group and told him not to miss it. Her voice was shaking when she said it.

He sat alone in silence, not quite believing what he was seeing. Could boys grow hair that long? Was it possible? And why in the world would they want to? Their names flashed over their faces: Ringo Starr, Paul McCartney, George Harrison, and—lastly—John Lennon. Beneath his name was the heartbreaking news: (Sorry, girls, he's married.)

The phone rang.

"Belson residence. John speaking."

"Are you watching this?" asked the familiar voice of Jeff Womack.

"Of course. What d'ya think?"

"I think I'm wearing my hair combed down over my forehead like that to school tomorrow."

"Bet you a dollar you don't."

"In that case, say good-bye to Mr. Washington."

"You say good-bye. I'm hanging up so I can watch the rest of the show."

"Well, before you do that, answer me one question. Are you going to ask Michelle to the Valentine's dance this weekend?"

John hesitated. "I don't wanna talk about it."

"Why not? I thought you stayed to talk to her on Friday."
"I said I don't wanna talk about it."
"But I'm your friend. You can tell me about these things."
"I'm hanging up now."
"But . . ."
"Bye."

And then something remarkable occurred. John was suddenly and miraculously caught up in the only part of the Beatles that mattered—their music. As they sang the lyrics to "I Want To Hold Your Hand," a transformation took place in John's spirit. Visibly moved, his eyes moist, he listened intently. They were singing about *him*, about his feelings toward Michelle. For, more than anything else in the world, John wanted to hold Michelle's hand, to walk side by side down the halls of Miller Junior High School with fingers interlocked as if to shout to all of his peers: "Look at me! I'm not lonely anymore! When I touch her, I feel happy inside! And it doesn't matter what any of you think of her, or me, or us!"

John's next not-so-courageous thoughts pushed him toward panic. Would he be able to break through the protective wall she had erected around herself? Would she allow him inside as she had that day when the rubber snake had forced her to let down her guard?

The shrieks from the TV shook him back to reality. The four boys from Liverpool surrounded Ed Sullivan. And, as they alternately shook his hand and waved to the delirious crowd, it was hard to figure out who was happier. But one young viewer, soaked with joyous sweat at having been shown the way to real love, was awfully happy that Ed had invited the group to play on his show that evening.

***

Jeff Womack was true to his word. He appeared the following day in Mrs. Roman's first-hour class with his dark hair combed down over his forehead in emulation of a Beatle haircut. The girls went crazy. Mrs. Roman went crazy too, sending Jeff to the boys' room to fix his hair. While he was gone, she lectured the class regarding real music versus electronic noise, creating some tension among the girls.

"I believe you owe me some cash," said Jeff as he casually took his seat.

"You know what hurts more than this?" whispered John as he slapped a dollar bill into his friend's eager hand. "It's that now you're more popular than ever."

"Some of us have it; some of us don't."

The Beatles had it. Beatlemania swept through the school that day like an all-consuming earthquake, swallowing sanity in its wake. Kids talked about little else, and by lunchtime, Jeff's stunt had gained him another notch on his legendary belt. Girls let it be known that they were desperately available for the weekend dance and would be thrilled to be seen with the Beatlesque boy. He had but to choose.

"Tater tots, please."

The grumpy woman scooped up six potato nuggets as if they were precious gems. She dumped them next to the meatloaf and green beans on Jeff's Styrofoam tray. John, next in line, chose mashed potatoes instead. The gravy settled like a volcanic lake atop the lump of white starch.

Jeff glanced over his shoulder. "You shoulda taken the tater tits."

John's annoyance at his friend's condescending demeanor continued to build. It was as if Jeff had a clue about this boy-girl thing looming like a tornado on the horizon ahead of them. As if he understood what John was still trying to grasp—that the Beatles had just upped the ante.

"By the way, Ringo, or whatever it is you call yourself these days, I thought you might like to know that I'm asking Michelle to the Valentine's dance."

They were seated across from each other at their usual table. It was here that they had hashed out problems in the past, helping each other negotiate the deceptive maze of junior high. John felt instantly relieved that he said it out loud, an affirmation of the pledge he had made to himself the night before. He didn't expect Jeff's quick answer.

"Not a good idea."

Now what? thought John. "Excuse me?"

"You heard me. Ask Gail Swanson. She's hot to go with you."

"What are you talking about? Just last night on the phone, if I remember correctly, you were hounding me to ask Michelle."

"That was before I had a little chat with Gail at her locker before school this morning. She's been thinking about you since her party. She really wants you to ask her to the dance. She thinks you look like John Lennon."

John froze. A dry piece of meatloaf slid off the end of his fork. John Lennon? This was flattery of the highest order, being compared to a Beatle when it was the only thing every boy in school suddenly wanted to be.

"She said that?"

"She did indeed."

John sighed heavily and set his fork down. His appetite was gone. This was a dilemma of exquisite proportion. Gail Swanson was not only very attractive and incredibly sweet, but she was also part of the in-crowd. A date with her would be a sign of approval for John. He would no longer be the four-eyed, book-loving chess player. He would be the cool kid who looked like a Beatle and who twisted and shouted with a girl who, only a year earlier, was completely out of his league.

On the other hand, he had promised himself to pursue Michelle, whom he wanted to get to know. But she was cold to him. And with her problem . . . well, she most likely wouldn't be allowed to go to the dance anyway. And Gail wouldn't wait all week.

"Gail won't wait all week, you know. If you don't ask her soon, someone else will."

John caved. "Okay, I'll do it."

"Good." Jeff paused. "Oh, and not that you care, but I'm asking Lori Tortello."

So, after much hesitation and an urgent trip to the bathroom, John picked up the phone that night to call Gail Swanson. Before he finally dialed her number, he experienced terrifying flashbacks of the "Nancy Olson incident," as it had come to be known. He worried that Jeff might have incorrectly assessed Gail's feelings and that she would only put him down with some flimsy excuse or outright lie. But, as it turned out, the only thing he had to fear was . . .

"Hello, Gail? This is John Belson, and I was wondering if—"

"John, did you see them on TV last night?" And she was off and running.

For the next fifteen minutes, John said little. Gail, however, said much. Apparently, she had been reading up on the boys in *16* and *Tiger Beat*. "And George's favorite actress is Elizabeth Taylor and—oh, guess what?—he loves lamb chops. And Paul hates to shave. He calls it the curse of mankind. And—you're not going to believe this—he can play the drums, just like Ringo. But did you know that Ringo is just a stage name? His real name is Richard Starkey."

By the time she stopped to take a breath, John had almost forgotten why he'd called her. "Uh, Gail, would you like to go to the Valentine's dance with me?"

"Oh, John, I'd love to. Thanks for asking me."

John braced for the "but"—such as, "But I can't because my Uncle Jonas and Aunt Cecilia are coming to stay with us for the weekend," *or* "But I can't because my dog Clover has been very sick lately, and I'm afraid he might die."

It never came.

"I'll see you tomorrow at school, okay? And don't forget, Beatles forever. Bye."

Well, that was easy, thought John. For some reason, his head hurt.

***

Later that week, Gail and he agreed to meet at the dance, a fairly common practice. So, throwing all caution—and sanity—to the wind, John seized upon a wild idea with which to surprise her. After an entire, ear-shattering week of listening to every girl in school talk incessantly about the Beatles, John had come to the obvious conclusion that anything "Beatle" would enhance his reputation—such as it was—with the opposite sex. He had only to reflect on the past Monday morning, when Jeff had worn the mop-top look to first hour, to appreciate the group's inherent power over young girls. These giggling goddesses had run their slender fingers through his friend's hair in shameful, orgy-like fashion. And the sheer magic of the moment had not been missed. If the Beatles were able to thrust Jeff into the spotlight with such dramatic flair, what might they do for him?

And so, John sat alone at his kitchen table only hours before the dance with the necessary materials set out before him. Thin, black ties were the look of the era. Thin, navy blue ties were worn on less formal occasions. The tie that adorned the boy's table, however, bore no resemblance to early 1960s chic. This tie, discovered by lucky accident in the attic, belonged to John's father, who had worn it in his youth. It had apparently come from Mars. It was very wide, colored in different shades of pink and purple, and had egg-shaped designs alternating down the front with swirling, *Twilight Zone*-like circles. With a little work . . .

Other items on the table included model paint, black yarn, electrical tape, scissors, glue, and a magazine devoted entirely to pictures and stories of the Fab Four. Working quickly, John flipped through the pages. There . . . perfect, but then, this really wasn't his doing. Four faces, each slightly larger than the one before. Ringo on top, the smallest face for the narrowest part of the tie, placed directly over one of the oval designs. George next, larger, below Ringo. John next. Finally, at the bottom, Paul, covering the largest expanse of tie. The excited boy glued the faces in place. Neatly cut the yarn. Taped it over the smiling images so it hung just above their eyes, loose so it flopped up and down like real hair. Painted bright green guitars between John and Paul; green and white musical notes everywhere; an orange snare drum next to Ringo.

The creation was completed in record time. John had turned an already bizarre tie into something magical, something mystical, something beyond belief. Like Dr. Frankenstein's monster, this baby could turn some heads.

For once in his life, John had not miscalculated. For once, he had foreseen the wonderful, beautiful reaction to his unique choice of dress. The evening witnessed his transformation from miserable obscurity into Cinderella at the ball. Gorgeous girls who had never spoken to him—never even noticed him in the hallway—stumbled on high heels trying to cut in on his increasingly jealous date for at least one dance. At one point, Gail pressed herself tightly against his chest, crushing the homemade tie between them.

Jeff Womack could only stand by the punch bowl and shake his head in wonder at how the night had turned out. His date, the delectable Lori Tortello, had called in sick, forcing him to come stag to the dance. He slouched along with the other solos and pondered the wiles of fate. It did not appear that the chaperones were going to send John home for his inappropriate attire, allowing the beaming boy to live out his fantasy. Jeff, therefore, would have to be content hanging out in the company of wannabees, biding time by passing gas and telling bawdy jokes.

Meanwhile, back on the dance floor, the night belonged to the newly popular John Belson.

11

It didn't take long for the magic to wear off. Monday morning, his talisman tucked safely away in a dresser drawer, John rediscovered the meaning of dull routine. In the crowded hallways, girls swept past him, a shattered pumpkin by the side of the road. Bill Dobbs stopped by his locker only to brag about slipping out of the dance with Gloria Stevens and finding a darkened hallway, where they made out. Even Gail—who had given him a hug and told him she'd had a wonderful time when her parents picked her up from the dance—was refocused on the important things in life. She and her friends sat a lunch table away from John and spoke in incredibly loud voices about the Beatles' second consecutive Sunday with Ed, this one broadcast live from Miami the previous night. John's head began to hurt again, much as it had while listening to Gail on the phone the other night.

"Hello, lover boy," said Jeff, dropping his tray to the table. "Welcome to another Meatloaf Monday."

"Where have you been? I thought you were out sick."

"I was. Sick of school, that is. I convinced my mom I had a sore throat, so she let me sleep in. How was the morning without me?"

"Boring. Mr. Schwartz beat us up with comma usage. And then Miss Parras assigned us a new dialogue about some French kids learning to ski."

"Figures. Those Frenchies are snobs. You don't see any of us poor kids skiing, do you?"

It was true, thought John. He had never skied in his life.

"Speaking of French," Jeff continued, "did Gail Swanson give you a nighty-night kiss after the dance?"

"No," John answered somewhat defensively. "She hugged me though."

"I'm surprised she didn't kiss your tie. She spent more time looking at it than at you."

"Dry up," said John, stabbing angrily at his green beans.

"I'm serious. Half of those girls just go to the dance so they can be seen. I think Gail's one of them."

"Last week you said she was hot for me."

"Maybe I exaggerated."

"Or maybe, just maybe, you're jealous because your date told you she was sick. Who knows? Maybe she had a sore throat just like yours."

Jeff scowled. "Okay, believe what you want. But I bet she won't even dance with you after lunch in the gym."

"Why wouldn't she?"

"I don't know. Because she doesn't want to be seen as going steady, perhaps? Think about it. Maybe she'd prefer to be popular with everyone."

John glanced over at Gail's table. She was holding court. Her friends eagerly soaked up her exclamations about what was happening with the Beatles. "And they're going back to England to make their own movie!"

Vivian Fay, a pretty, doe-eyed girl whom John had known since kindergarten, put her hands up to her ears, shook her head violently, and screamed.

Then, laughing and shouting, they all rose as one and made their way across the cafeteria to co-mingle with some boys from the basketball team.

Jeff smiled. "I rest my case."

Exasperated, John stared into Jeff's eyes. "Shut up. Please, just shut up."

"Okay. I've gotta go pee. Catch ya later."

John's head was now throbbing, and his stomach was queasy. He thought for a passing moment that he might throw up. He looked around the cafeteria and realized that he was quite alone. Had Saturday night been a dream? Had he just imagined—or wanted to believe so badly—that girls, especially Gail, actually liked him?

"I heard you were the prince of the ball." The voice was so close to John that it startled him. He looked up quickly into the soft eyes of Michelle Watson. She was smiling. He opened his mouth to speak, but no words came out.

"May I sit down?"

Suddenly remembering his manners, John lurched to his feet, banging his knee on the hard metal underside of the table. He gritted his teeth, his face a mask of pain.

Michelle laughed. "Oh, I'm sorry. Are you all right?"

"Yeah, I'm fine," John assured her. He fell back down into his seat and resisted the urge to rub his injury.

She sat across from him in the spot Jeff had vacated. "I overheard some of the girls talking in Mrs. Danforth's class this morning. Wild tie, huh?"

John grimaced. "I guess."

"Well, they made it sound like it was all quite fun."

"I suppose," said John, staring at the table.

Michelle sensed his sullenness. "What's wrong?"

Everything, thought John. But when he looked up into Michelle's face, clouded with concern, it seemed more like everything was right, as if all the planets had suddenly aligned.

Before John could answer, before he could thank Michelle for stopping by and saving his topsy-turvy day, the cafeteria monitor's voice, greatly enhanced by a bullhorn, cut him off. "Okay, boys and girls, make sure your tables are cleared off and all garbage is thrown into one of the receptacles! Then, line up at the doors for the short walk to the girls' gym! Let's hold the noise down now!"

"See you in choir," said Michelle, reaching out quickly and touching his hand. And then, like a white, windblown cloud in a sun-soaked sky, she drifted away to join the multitude.

The following week, John's skies darkened again.

***

"And why, exactly, did you think it was a good idea to throw snowballs in the hallway?" It was déjà vu all over again. John and Jeff sat in the familiar chairs and looked across the desk at a visibly upset Mr. Carver. The boys had thrown said snowballs a week earlier, having scooped them up in the courtyard while passing through on their way to gym. And they were a bit surprised that it had only now been brought to the assistant principal's attention.

"Do you know how I found out about this?"

"No, sir," said John softly, staring at a coffee stain on the carpet.

"Well, I'll tell you. I hauled two sixth-grade boys in here earlier today for pelting some poor girl standing by her locker. They said they were sorry and that they'd gotten the idea from observing those "older boys" Womack and Belson. It's a clear case of monkey-see, monkey-do. The problem is, as supposedly mature upperclassmen, you're supposed to be setting a positive example for the youngsters in the building."

Actually, the real problem was that John was regressing. There had been a fleeting moment when he had reached out for the baton of maturity, when it seemed like—if he could just hold himself together—he would smoothly transition into the mainstream social structure of the school. But, angry with the flighty girls who alternately embraced and rejected him, he had hurled the baton to the ground and veered aimlessly off the track once again. And the wayward Jeff Womack was more than happy to lead him in that direction.

The one-week detention imposed upon them was no big deal. Show up after school; do some homework or read a book; call for a ride home. Mr. Carver didn't seem to care enough to try to save them anymore. And Mr. Schwartz only belittled them when they returned to LASS, suggesting they bring playpens from home to set up in his classroom.

But, as bad as all this might have seemed, none of it compared to what happened in choir that same day.

It most likely occurred because John was slowly evolving into someone he wasn't meant to be. As he approached Mrs.

Roman's sanctuary, he stewed over his apparent death wish in continuing to ignore common sense whenever Jeff suggested something sinister or stupid, such as the snowballs. And when he took his place beside his misguided friend halfway up the risers, he was in no mood to be distracted from the task at hand.

"These songs are simply not coming together," a tense Mrs. Roman admonished the choir. "It's less than two weeks until the concert. We must work harder."

Okay, thought John. If that's what you want, then I'll work harder. But his heart wasn't in it. The fact that he had been pulled out of chess club to be in the dopey choir was still a daily irritant to him. And it certainly hadn't brought him any closer to Michelle as he had once dreamed it would.

He glanced over at her. She was the biggest mystery of all. Since that day a week ago in the cafeteria when she had boldly approached and comforted him, she had again withdrawn into her private world. And, although he had wanted to walk across the gym floor and ask her to dance every single day, he could not summon the nerve. He knew she was a pariah, and it still mattered to him what Gail Swanson and the other socialites thought of him. Clearly, his mind was muddled.

Without warning, John felt the sharp stab of Jeff's elbow in his ribs. "Move over, will ya?"

Anger rose like bile, and John shoved back with his shoulder. "You move over."

The push was harder than intended, and Jeff, attempting to steady himself, lost his balance and fell onto the wooden risers with a loud crash. The tight-knit, focused group of singers fell apart with laughter.

Mrs. Roman went off like a cherry bomb. "That's it! Out! Both of you! Leave my choir and report to study hall! Now!"

John and Jeff stumbled awkwardly off the risers and toward the exit, flashing hate stares at each other while Mrs. Roman continued to berate them. "Shame on you! I knew I shouldn't have allowed you in! Now we're short two tenors."

The last line, spoken softer than the others, was directed to no one in particular. Hopelessness had invaded her world.

The trek to study hall was both long and silent, neither boy willing to continue the warfare.

John pulled a Poe volume off the shelves and began reading the lurid prose. He attempted to convince himself it was inevitable that he would end up here, although he didn't relish the thought of having to tell his parents he'd been kicked out of choir for horsing around. It wouldn't matter to his working-class father that John didn't want to be part of it in the first place; it would only matter that his folks were looking forward to the concert and that he didn't finish the job.

Like the narrator in "The Black Cat," whose inability to control his drinking led to the abuse and eventual murder of his wife, John was sliding rapidly downhill into a chasm of his own creation. And—he came to understand in that solitary moment of contemplation—there was only one way out.

Three steps would need to be taken. Step #1: divorce Jeff. Their friendship was now like a marriage on the brink of death; there was simply no point in trying to resurrect it. John would still eat lunch with him, but that was it. Step #2: reclaim his own personality. He was who he was, and if the Gail Swansons of the school didn't like it, they could lump it. Step #3: ask Michelle out. Maybe, John thought, he was so miserable because he hadn't yet done this when he knew in his heart that she would be the key to his salvation.

12

Wednesday morning, seven o'clock. John slammed his mom's car door shut and headed up the slushy walkway toward the school's front entrance. Two inches of wet, heavy snow had fallen the night before, and overcast skies, threatening to dump some more, hung somberly above him.

"Damn it!" John yelled to no one as he slipped and almost fell. "Where the hell is Arvid?"

Arvid was the school's janitor. With the buses due by seven-thirty, he should have been out shoveling the wide expanse of pavement. But instead, John decided, the old man must be hiding out in his congested little closet, lighting up that first cigarette of the day. And with all those flammable chemicals stacked on the shelves, his nicotine habit might just blow the whole school to smithereens someday. But Arvid, grizzled and worn from years of mopping up puke and scraping obscenities off of desks, wasn't too concerned about that. In fact, John surmised, he probably wasn't too concerned about anything. If some poor kid cracked his skull open from a nasty fall, Arvid would just shrug his shoulders and say in his thick Swedish accent, "Vat's a body to do? Da Lord made da snow come down."

John hurried to his locker, shed his coat and gloves, and walked steadily toward Michelle's locker. He had lied to his mom and asked her to drop him off early for more-of-the-same math help. His intended purpose, before the halls filled, was to meet Michelle and ask her out. Simple, yet terrifying.

For the next ten minutes, John stood with his back frozen to her locker. He wiped sweat off his brow and chewed his fingernails to nubs, all the while carefully rehearsing his lines. He hadn't seen her since Monday—that awful day when he had been kicked out of choir—and he wasn't sure how he would be received.

When he heard the slam of the entrance door from the floor below, he almost bolted. But, by then, it was too late. He stood facing the stairway and listened to her footfalls coming slowly up the steps. He took one last deep breath before she stepped into the deserted hallway.

"Oh," she said, "you startled me for a second." She laughed, regaining her composure. "What are you doing here so early?"

Ignoring her question, John launched into his prepared script. "Hello, Michelle. I was wondering if you'd like to go to a movie with me on Friday night?"

Her eyes showed no surprise, almost as if she had expected to be asked. Well, John thought, he *had* delayed it for a long time. She threw him off balance, however, with her answer.

"Maybe. What's playing?" She walked past him and casually opened her locker.

John searched the air for words. "Uh . . . I don't know." Recovering quickly, he added, "It's a new one Friday. I'll have to look it up."

The downtown movie theatre changed films once a week, the current one running through Thursday. John was annoyed with both himself for not knowing and Michelle for bothering to ask.

She turned to face him. "I'm not sure," she teased. "Do you think I should go out with such a rowdy boy? I mean, getting kicked out of choir and all . . ."

John swallowed hard. "That was stupid. I'm sorry it happened. I'll understand if you say—"

"Yes."

"Yes?"

"Yes. I'd love to go. And I don't really care what's playing."

John, overwhelmed by light-headedness, felt he might faint on the spot. He placed a hand firmly against a locker to steady himself. "Great," he said, genuinely relieved. But now came the hard part. "Look, is it okay if we meet there?

It's just that I don't want my parents to know I have a date. They're pretty strict, and they might not approve. I'm gonna tell them I'm meeting some friends at the theatre. They'll drop me off." As if to sweeten the pot, he added, "We can go for ice cream after the show."

Michelle smiled. "Sure. I live close enough to walk. Even in the cold."

A pang of guilt stabbed at John. What kind of romantic was he, anyhow, allowing his date to trudge through a frozen wasteland for the privilege of meeting Mr. Wonderful at the movies?

"Don't worry. I walk here every day. I enjoy being outdoors."

"Okay, I mean, if you're sure. I'll find out what's playing and let you know tomorrow."

***

John Belson had a secret. He was taking Michelle Watson, the nicest, sweetest, prettiest girl on the planet, to the movies on Friday night, and he vowed not to tell a single soul. Not his parents, who would interrogate him like trained FBI agents until he coughed up all the facts about her and her family. Not Jeff Womack, who would make snide comments or—worse—try to turn it into yet another disastrous double date. Not Bill Dobbs, who would cheapen John's thrill by giving him make-out tips. Not Gail Swanson, who would laugh in his face and never speak to him again because he had chosen to be a loser instead of clinging desperately to the fringes of the popular group she headed.

No, this time John was not going to do anything to ruin his happiness. This time he was going to do it the right way.

Later that same day when John arrived home from school, he strode across the street to the home of Steve Daniels. Steve was two years John's senior and, years before, had condescended to play with the younger boy on occasion. But by the time Steve had gone off to junior high, the age gap between the boys was too large, and they barely spoke to each other. The last time they'd had any type of conversation, John recalled, was almost a year ago. Steve had been walking home from high school near the end of his freshman year and had seen John cutting the lawn.

"Hey, Belson!" Steve shouted over the clatter of the push mower.

John stopped in his tracks, the mower's blades whirring to a sudden halt.

"Since when do you wear glasses?"

"Since two years ago."

"Oh," said Steve, continuing on his way without another word.

But John was desperate. He knew that Steve was an usher on weekends at the theatre, and he needed to ask him what was playing on Friday night. He rang the doorbell and waited.

"What do you want, Belson?" said the less-than-neighborly boy upon opening the door.

"Uh . . ." The hesitation in John's voice came from the genuine fear of his one-time childhood companion. It was true they had never been best friends, but Steve had once been a genial kid, one who liked to shoot marbles and play baseball with others on the block. Over the years, he had slowly evolved into a sullen boy who looked down on John and his friends.

Now, he stood staring out from the shadows, irritation clouding his pale face. He raised a half-eaten banana to show John. "I'm eating here. Can I help you with something?" The last line was spoken with as much scorn as was humanly possible.

"Yeah, as a matter of fact, I know you work at the show and uh . . . well, I was just wondering if you could tell me what was playing starting this Friday?"

Steve snorted. "What do I look like, a newspaper?"

"Well, I thought . . ."

"You thought, did you?" Again, the snort. "You know, I was having a good day until I came to the door and found you on the other side." A brief pause. "But, okay. If you promise to go away, I'll tell you."

"I promise."

Steve stared at him with contempt. He took a bite of the banana and chewed slowly.

John's patience was waning. He didn't need this. What had he ever done to be treated with such loathing?

"*The Haunting.*"

"What?"

"I said, *The Haunting*. That's the name of the movie."

"What's it about?"

Steve rolled his eyes. "It's about a haunted house. Scary stuff." He smiled a silver smile, his mouth a mass of metal. "You'll probably pee your pants."

Before John could respond, the door shut in his face.

Walking home from his encounter with Steve, John wondered how their once-friendly relationship had disintegrated into nothingness. It seemed to have much to do with the fact that Steve had already been in high school for two years and looked at John as unworthy of his attention. After all, two years difference in age meant little when younger kids were rounding up players for a pick-up game of baseball at the school playground; those couple of years meant everything when the older one was trying to fit in with his new peers.

John marched directly to the phone on the kitchen wall. He wasn't sure Michelle would like a horror movie, and he thought it best to call her right away.

It was only when he stared in confusion at the circle of numbers staring back from the black face of the phone that it hit him. He had no idea what Michelle's number was. It wouldn't be in the phone book either; she was too new in town. "Crap-o-la," he said, placing the receiver back. Feeling a headache spreading forward from his temples, he reached into the cabinet for the aspirin bottle, took two with a glass of water, and finally removed his winter coat. He slipped past his mom, who was vacuuming the living room carpet, and slid into the sanctuary of his bedroom.

Other than sitting through a barrage of annoying questions from his parents at dinner—"How's school? How's Jeff? Are you doing any better in math?"—and providing monosyllabic responses to them—"Okay. Fine. Yes."—John spent the entire evening listening to Ron Riley's show on WLS via his transistor radio. Beatles songs were still receiving the majority of airplay, but another English group, the Dave Clark Five, was pounding its way up the charts with a song called "Glad All Over." The British Invasion was underway.

John closed his eyes and let the songs wash in waves over his tired body. They carried him gently to a magical place where never-before-realized feelings of love sprung into the open like a newborn from its womb. His nascent thoughts journeyed outward to caress Michelle's hair; her eyes beckoned to him. He fell asleep, fully clothed, and slept soundly until morning.

Throughout the next day, he tolerated the mundane affairs swirling about him—the familiar faces, voices, bells—until he could meet Michelle at her locker. Even lunchtime, with Jeff at his hilarious best carving out a food sculpture of Mrs. Roman—a mound of white rice for her beehive hairdo and lumpy red potatoes for her mammoth breasts—failed to arouse him from his trance. Glimpses of Michelle across the crowded cafeteria and the segregated gym floor only caused more anxiety to creep into his brain. What if she changed her mind?

When the day's final bell sounded, John panted doglike toward Michelle's locker. They arrived simultaneously.

"Hi," he said, only slightly out of breath.

"Hi to you."

"I wanted you to know I found out what movie's playing tomorrow night. It's called *The Haunting*. It's supposed to be real scary, so if you don't want to go . . ."

"I like scary movies. Unless you're afraid?"

"No, I . . . no, of course not."

"Besides," Michelle added, "I loved the book when I read it."

This was news to John. He considered himself a voracious reader, yet he had never heard of this novel. "The book?"

"Yes, the book. It's called *The Haunting of Hill House*. It was written by a woman named Shirley Jackson. It's a very eerie story, so you may have to hold me."

John felt his head fill with helium until he almost lifted off the floor.

Recovering, he blurted out, "So, I'll meet you in front of the theatre at 7:00, okay?"

The evening show always began promptly at 7:30. The early rendezvous would allow them time to purchase popcorn or candy and find good seats.

"Sounds good." And she was gone.

13

The Royale stood proud. The ancient brick building and its gravel parking lot took up an entire block. Its front entrance, with its ticket booth, thick glass doors, and massive marquee, beckoned passersby to come in from the cold and relax for a couple of hours. The only movie theatre in town, it had no competition. After films such as *West Side Story* and *Lawrence of Arabia* had finished their runs at the giant palaces in Chicago, they would turn up here and at other suburban locations six months or even a year later. Kids didn't mind; the films were all new to them.

    John stood blowing cold smoke from his mouth. He had been dropped off early and had already waited for twenty minutes. Occasionally, he patted his arms with his gloves or stamped his boots on the frozen sidewalk. He prayed his date wasn't having problems walking to meet him. He should have just bitten the bullet and had his parents pick her up. But then he would have had to weather the storm of their prying questions about her. And if they learned that she didn't have a father around or that her mother was an alcoholic, what then? John shivered. Should he just buy the tickets and stand inside where it was warm?

    At precisely 7:05—John had been checking his watch every thirty seconds—Michelle turned the corner and waved to him. Walking past the coming-attractions posters that stared out from the sunken windows, she approached the delighted boy. She looked radiant. Her black hair crept out from beneath a green knit hat and shimmered in the lights of the marquee. Her soft, brown eyes searched his face, and a bright smile broke across hers. "You look frozen," she said. "Your face is all red."

"Nah, I'm fine," John lied. "It's not that cold out." He pulled two dollars from his wallet and said, "Wait here. I'll get the tickets."

Minutes later, a welcome blast of hot air enveloped their bodies as they entered the Royale's lobby. A short line had formed through a tunnel of velvet ropes, and the couple joined the surge.

"Oh, no," moaned John, staring toward the front of the line.

"What is it?"

"It's Steve. He's the ticket taker."

"Who is he?"

"Nobody. He's just my neighbor. But he hates me. He hates everybody."

"Oh, that can't be true. You're exaggerating."

"Wait and see."

John inched warily toward the older boy's post and handed him the two tickets. Steve, looking ridiculous in his usher's cap and jacket—burgundy with bronze braids and buttons—tore them in half without looking up. "Enjoy the show," he mumbled through his braces. Only then did he lift his head, a spark of recognition flaring up in his eyes. "Well, hello, Belson." His gaze shifted to Michelle, and he quickly appraised her. Looking back at John, he said in a flat, matter-of-fact voice, "Move along, please. You're holding up the line."

When they were safely out of earshot, John turned to his date and said, "You see what I mean?"

"Not really," laughed Michelle. "He seemed polite to me."

"It's his job to be polite. But that was only on the surface. Underneath he was smirking at us."

Michelle laughed again. "Smirking?"

"Smirking. And he was studying you, judging you."

"Oh, yeah? Well, how did I measure up?"

"That's obvious, isn't it? He saw how sharp you looked and wondered how such a nice-looking girl could go out with someone like me. And that's when he smirked at me—at us."

"Underneath his polite exterior?"

"Yes."

"Well, then, I really should go back and tell him what I think. That I'm very happy going out with you, and that he should keep his undercover smirks to himself."

John was thunderstruck. Who was this delightful girl?

She winked at him. "Don't let him annoy you. We're here to have fun, remember?"

"Yes, of course," said John, shaking himself back to reality. "Would you like some popcorn?"

"I thought you'd never ask."

***

They sat huddled in the plush seats, their winter coats scrunched behind them. The thirty-cent box of buttered popcorn sat balanced between them. That and the ten-cent cups of orange soda they held kept their hands busy. This was a momentary relief for John, who did not yet have to worry about where he would place his hands and arms once the picture began. But he had spent the last two days thinking about it.

This was the curse of being the male of the species in the pre-sexual revolution years. Guys were the ones who always had to make the first move. They were the ones who crossed the expanse of gym floor to request a dance; they were the ones who tracked girls like spies through crowded hallways looking for the perfect moment to ask them out; they were the ones who were expected to boldly lean in for that first touch, that first kiss; they were the ones who presented the going-steady pin and the engagement ring, but only after asking the father's permission to marry. Marry?

John was sweating profusely. His breathing was ragged. His thoughts had shot ahead of him and produced a panic. He took his hand out of the popcorn box, reached into his pants pocket, and pulled out a handkerchief. With it, he wiped the perspiration from his brow. "Whoa, it's hot in here."

Michelle smiled. "Not really," she said.

John paused. He quickly shoved the damp handkerchief back into his pocket. "Maybe it just seems warm."

Stupid, stupid, stupid, he thought. He began to coach himself. Relax. Breathe in. Breathe out. Sip the soda. Swallow easy. Breathe in. Breathe out. The house lights dimmed. The curtain opened. Coming attractions filled the screen. Peter Sellers. Angela Lansbury. Young girls pursuing a famous concert pianist. John knew that Michelle liked him or else she wouldn't be there. What, then, was his next move?

In the next second, she shifted her weight toward him, slid her arm beneath his, and intertwined her slender fingers with his own. She then dropped her head onto his shoulder. Well, John concluded, that was easy. It seemed to him that, whatever fears he harbored about this relationship, Michelle clearly did not share them. Her friendly demeanor and casual body language suggested to him that she trusted him, felt safe with him. And he vowed not to rush things, to let life take its course, to enjoy each moment.

This would have been easier had the movie not scared the daylights out of John. Its plot was simple. A parapsychologist enticed a few people to spend some time with him in Hill House to see if anything weird might happen. It did. Directed by the legendary Robert Wise, the film succeeded without once showing a ghost or demon or anything else. Rather, terror was created in the minds of audience members through skillful use of black-and-white photography, bizarre camera angles, and eerie sound effects. By the time Julie Harris' character, the timid Eleanor, arrived early in the movie and was warned by Mrs. Dudley, a very spooky caretaker, that no one would hear her if she screamed "in the night, in the dark," John was ready to sacrifice his dream date and flee this nightmare.

"What's the matter?" whispered Michelle. "You're all tense."

John realized he was sitting upright, Michelle's head no longer on his shoulder, her fingers no longer locked in his. "Hello, I'm scared," he admitted. "Aren't you?"

"It's just a movie."

Oh, great, thought John. He was ready to run screaming from the building, and his date had nerves of steel. He guessed she would probably never consent to go out with him again.

Desperately trying to appear relaxed, John slumped down in his chair and wondered if this had all been a big mistake. Maybe. But he knew one thing for certain. He didn't understand girls. Not a clue. He'd always been told that they turned into pudding during a scary movie, that they whimpered like frightened puppies and cried out to be held. But not this girl. Not Michelle the myth-buster.

On the screen, the house's permanent inhabitants had written on the wall; they wanted Eleanor to come home. John wanted to *be* home.

"Hold me." John was jerked from his terrified state. Michelle reached over, grabbed John's arm, and placed it across her shoulders. His hand felt the softness of her sweater, and he squeezed tightly. She snuggled up against him, their bodies melting into one.

They stayed that way for the remainder of the movie. Whether she, too, was frightened or was merely playing a part, John could not be sure. Nor did he care. For this was the moment he had dreamed of for a long time. He had been waiting for a girl to complement—no, to complete him. To make him whole. To drive away the sick feeling that he might always be alone.

When Eleanor died at the film's climax, it seemed natural to feel sorry for her. But John didn't. Her life had been one of abject loneliness, and now she was at peace. The house had wanted her—had claimed her—and now she would never despair again.

The subdued crowd made its way slowly up the aisle. The couple disentangled themselves, the blood draining down into John's lifeless arm.

"Still scared?" asked Michelle.

"Maybe."

They stood.

"Well," continued John, "you'll have to admit it was a tad unsettling."

"Only for the weak-minded," she teased.

They went up the aisle and stepped into the bright lobby. John glanced up at the giant clock behind the concession counter. It read 9:35.

"What time do you have to be home?"

"My mom usually says eleven. But I've come in later."

John hesitated. "Did you tell her you were meeting a boy?"

"I did. She didn't mind. I've gone out with boys before."

This was a revelation that floored John. But then he quickly realized that he knew absolutely nothing about Michelle's past. "I promised you ice cream. Would you like to walk to Petersen's Drug Store? It's only a block away."

"I don't think so. I'm still full from the popcorn, and besides, it's pretty cold out there."

So, then, this was it. The end of the date. John's heart dipped. He wanted it to go on forever. "Well, then," he heard himself say, "why don't you let me walk you home? I can zip back here afterward and call my folks."

It was Michelle's turn to hesitate. "If you're sure it won't be too much of a bother."

"Not at all."

She hesitated again. "Maybe my mom will still be up, and you can meet her."

Did either of them want this?

"Okay."

The still night had become blustery, and the wind cut deeply into their cheeks. Simultaneously, they slipped their arms around each other's waists and moved rapidly along. They did not speak.

Once, Michelle lost her balance on a particularly treacherous stretch of sidewalk and tumbled to the ground, pulling John with her. They both laughed.

"Watch this," said Michelle. She stood, took a few steps onto the snow-clad lawn, and fell backward. "Snow angels." She flapped her arms up and down beside her.

John hurried to join her, exuberantly pumping his arms in a similar fashion. Climbing to their feet, they surveyed their handiwork.

"See, Mr. Robinson, I *can* create modern art!" John yelled into the wind.

Michelle pointed. "Yours looks crooked. A fallen angel, no doubt."

A porch light suddenly came to life, bathing the angels in sparkling splendor. A door slammed open.

"Hey, you kids, get off my lawn!"

The pair sprinted into the night, their hands and hearts locked in everlasting joy.

And it *was* to be everlasting. Many years later, John Belson would, in an instant, be able to call up the new emotions that had bubbled up inside of him that night. For he wasn't so much in love with Michelle as he was in love with the feelings he was experiencing for the first time in his life. And *those* he would never forget.

14

Out of breath, sharp daggers stabbing their lungs, the couple stopped beneath the eerie glow of a street lamp. John coughed twice. His chest hurt even more. "Whoa," he laughed, and another cough racked his body.

"Are you okay?" asked Michelle, still breathing heavily.

"Yeah, I'm fine. Boy, that guy was scarier than the ghosts of Hill House."

John laughed at his attempt at humor, but Michelle did not respond; she had become suddenly quiet.

"What's wrong?"

"It's just that real life is always scarier than make-believe." She turned to face him. "Sit down. I want to tell you something."

John lowered himself to the cold concrete of the curb. He leaned back and placed his gloved hands on the snow-covered parkway behind him. Michelle sat down next to him and turned her body sideways so she could look into his eyes.

"It's about my mother."

"I already know about your mother," ventured John.

"No, you don't. You only know what those people at school say. The ones who put everybody in a box and then label them so they can make their own lives seem better. I'm not a fool, John. I know what they say about me behind my back. I've been the new kid before."

"You mean . . ."

"Yeah, we've moved around a lot. I used to cry myself to sleep at night, but it doesn't seem to be worth the effort anymore. Either people like you for who you are or they don't."

"I like you," offered John.

"I know. And I like you. And if the other kids want to shut me out, I'll have to put up with that. But they should leave my mom out of it. She's a good person, but her life's been hard. She does the best she can for me, for us."

"She doesn't drink, then?"

"Sometimes. But it's not like they say, you know, like she's drunk all the time." She paused, deciding whether to say more. "My dad left us when I was five. I don't know why. Since then, we've never stayed in one place for long. So, I've never made any close friends. But she's got a good job this time. She works in an office, answering phones, typing, that sort of work. She hasn't missed a day."

"But Petey O'Neal said you stayed home all the time because your mom was . . . sick."

Michelle's eyes flashed with anger. "And you believed him?"

"Well, I thought . . ."

"No, you didn't think, or you would have considered the source. But I'm guessing you've had a sudden revelation. If my mom wasn't home, that means I've been staying home alone, faking sick notes to bring in the next day. Care to wonder why?"

John stared out toward the empty intersection. "I know why."

He flashed back to last year, recalling how he had pretended to be sick so he could stay home and watch game shows on TV, "Concentration" and "Truth or Consequences" a better hand than being mocked or ignored all day. He reflected on how he'd felt on those days when he had attended school, his loneliness weighing him down until he dragged along like a wounded soldier with battle fatigue. It was clear to him that Michelle had built a wall around herself to keep out that kind of pain, and it was up to John to break through it somehow.

"Well, you had better head back," stated Michelle. "I live a half block down; I can make it home from here. Besides, my mom's probably upstairs in her bedroom already. Reading."

John pushed himself up from the curb. His legs were numb from sitting in the cold, and he stamped his boots several times to revive his circulation. Then he reached down and gallantly pulled Michelle to her feet.

"Look," she said, her eyes softer now, "I meant what I said before. I like you. I think you're really nice. And I had a wonderful time tonight. So, if you want to go out again sometime . . ."

Her words trailed off, suspended delicately in the frigid air.

"I understand," said John. "Don't worry. I promise not to ask you to dance in the gym or anything."

Michelle smiled. "Will you come and see me in the concert next week?"

"Of course. Assuming Mrs. Roman lets me in the door."

They both laughed.

The next thing John knew Michelle's lips were barely brushing his cheek in a not-quite first kiss. When he recovered from what could only be described as blissful shock, he looked out over the suburban landscape to see this incredibly independent girl hurrying down the street toward her home. He stared in amazement at her retreating figure, hoping she would turn and wave at him. But, of course, she did not.

By himself—but no longer alone—John headed back to town. His thoughts were, for the most part, commonplace. First and foremost, he was sure he had fallen in love for the first time. And to justify this belief, he replayed the night over and over like a favorite sitcom. But, like Lucy and Ethel trying in vain to keep up with the candy-factory conveyor belt, he fumbled awkwardly over his fast-moving emotions. Michelle had been nice to him, warm and friendly, folding neatly into his arms in the comfy theatre seats. She had smiled at his nervousness, teased him about his fearfulness. Most importantly, she had been honest with him—about her mother's struggles, her father's flight, her fear of fitting in. She had asked nothing of him but to be himself. And she, in turn, would be herself. All in all, not a bad deal.

Secondly, he knew he wanted to marry this girl someday. But he was woefully inexperienced in the art of love, and therefore failed to comprehend that this would most likely never happen. Even Shakespeare's legendary Romeo was infatuated with Rosaline before he fell in love with and married Juliet. And if the ancient, star-crossed lovers had survived and gone on to produce nine children and eat boiled mutton for dinner twice a week, then Romeo would have spent endless hours wondering whatever happened to the comely Rosaline—while viewing Juliet through reality-coated lenses that showed her to be a little long in the tooth. It's always like that. Looking back across time, first love never grows old in the eyes of the lover, and thus remains "perfect" forever. And, right then, John truly believed that Michelle Watson was his perfect match. A match made in Heaven.

Then he saw them, the snow angels they had created in the angry man's yard. Side by side, they also looked perfect. With a devilish grin, John scooped up some snow, packed it into a solid ball, and threw it at the front door. Then he took off running, the cold wind at his back.

***

"So, I hear you took that new girl Michelle to the movies Friday night." Bill Dobbs had approached John from behind while he was bending over his locker scrabbling through papers in a hopeless attempt to find his math homework, which he thought he had completed Friday in study hall. (He hadn't.)

Wincing, John raised up his head. "Maybe. So what?" He had seen no one from school at the theatre, but apparently someone had seen him, or rather them. By now, the gossip would be spreading through the halls like a wildfire fanned by savage winds, each narrator adding a new twist to the story until the two innocents on a first date ended up having intercourse in the lobby.

"So, did you get any?"

John hesitated. Truth? Embellishment? He'd go with the truth. His life would turn out better that way. "It wasn't what I was after."

Bill looked genuinely surprised. Recovering quickly, he placed his large hand on John's shoulder. "Remember," he said in his most sincere voice, "you only have so much time to give to this endeavor. If she doesn't put out soon, move on to the next one. That's the best advice anyone will ever give you, my son."

John looked into the expressive eyes of the good-natured boy and wondered why he had ever thought he was cool. The irony, of course, was that Bill's pitching arm would assure him of ultra-cool jock status in high school, where some girls would sell their souls just to go out with him.

John bit his tongue to keep the "You're an idiot" from coming out. Instead, he smiled graciously and said, "Thanks. I'll keep that in mind."

Jeff was absent from Mr. Black's first-period shop class. The eighth graders were finished with their thirteen weeks of music and had moved on to practical arts. His absence meant that John didn't have to answer to the cynical boy, who would most likely adopt a negative attitude about the couple—if, indeed, that's what they were.

"It'll never work." Jeff had arrived just in time for lunch—again.

"Why not?"

"I just don't see a happy future for you, that's all."

"Oh, is that a fact? Now, let's see. First, you don't think Gail Swanson really likes me, and now, it's Michelle."

"I never said she didn't like you. Maybe she adores you. What I said was that it won't work out. She'll only hurt you in the end. And I'd hate to see that happen."

John glanced over at Michelle.

She was eating her lunch alone, an open paperback beside her tray.

"You see," Jeff said to illustrate. "She's alone, but she's content to be that way. My guess is she's lived a far different life than you have. Apples and oranges, you know."

John was speechless. All morning long, under a microscope, he had felt the inquisitive stares of his peers. They were weighing, judging, evaluating this new information about him—and her—and it made him feel very uncomfortable. Now, here he was, stuck in Philosophy 101, listening to the musings of a madman as he tried to dissect John's life like an embryo pig.

Under such pressure, he finally snapped. "What do you mean, 'It won't work out'? You know, lately it seems like you enjoy making others feel bad about themselves. Well, you know what? I don't feel bad about myself. In fact, I've never felt better. Thursday night I'm going to Mrs. Roman's concert to see Michelle perform her solo. And then I'm going to ask her out again. Do you want to know why? Because we like each other, that's why. And, who knows? Maybe it will work out just fine. Anything else?"

This time, Jeff was speechless.

***

John kept his promises to Michelle. He didn't ask her to dance in the gym, and he did show up at the concert. He was dressed nattily in a sport coat and normal tie. The songs, half-remembered, played through his mind as his eyes never left Michelle. In a white, knee-length dress, silken hair pulled back in a neat ponytail, she again looked angelic. Her solo was the highlight of the evening, earning her a standing ovation from the appreciative audience.

Afterward, John maneuvered his way through the crowd as it filed slowly into the adjoining area, which was set up for a reception with punch and cookies. Mrs. Roman, beaming like a sunflower, shot him a look as if to say, "See what you have missed?"

She was probably right, John concluded. If he hadn't behaved like such a fool, he could be basking in the well-deserved adulation that was being heaped on the choir by family and friends.

A group of adults surrounded Michelle, showering her with compliments. She smiled politely and thanked them for coming. John stood quietly nearby until only one woman remained with Michelle, and then he approached her.

"John," she said, her face lighting up even more as she acknowledged his presence. "Thanks for coming. Did you like it?"

"I did. You sang beautifully."

"John, I'd like you to meet someone. Mom, this is John Belson. John, this is my mother."

John, flung into panic, stuck his suddenly sweat-soaked palm out to her. "Very nice to meet you, Mrs. Watson."

"It's nice to meet you, John. Michelle told me she had a wonderful time with you the other night."

"Uh, yes," he stammered, "we did."

After some small talk, none of which John could recall five minutes later, they all said their good-byes.

Lying in bed, staring at the dark ceiling, John was excited. Michelle's mom seemed quite normal, and he hoped that the choir kids and their friends had seen her with Michelle and judged her to be no different than other moms. That was probably, John allowed himself to think, because no one had spiked the punch bowl.

15

March: the calendar's most boring month. Easter break was due in April, and then the eighth graders would head into the stretch. John and Michelle filled the time with a few more casual dates. They met in town several times, mostly at Petersen's Drug Store. There, sitting knee to knee at the long counter like a scene from *It's A Wonderful Life*, they sipped ice cream sodas and shared their personal likes and dislikes with each other. Michelle, John learned, loved classical music but admitted the Beatles were "cute," especially Paul. She liked to read novels but scorned television, which she considered a waste of time. She did love movies, however; she adored Audrey Hepburn and couldn't wait to see her in *My Fair Lady*. John told Michelle about his love for Sherlock Holmes stories, how he never missed an episode of "The Andy Griffith Show," and—on this particular day—promised to teach her how to play "the world's greatest game," chess.

"It's very challenging. The object of the game is to capture your opponent's king."

Michelle paused in mid-slurp, the lime liquid sliding back down through her straw. "Because he's the most powerful?"

"Actually, he's the weakest. The queen's the strongest."

Michelle's eyes danced. "I like this game already."

John smiled. "You see, the king can only move one space at a time, and he never goes on offense. The queen, the bishops, the knights, and the rooks attack by moving in different ways around the board."

"What's a rook?"

"A castle."

"The castle moves?"

"Only up and down the board. The bishops move diagonally, and the knights can jump over people. They're the only ones who can do that."

"On horseback?"

"In my set, they're just horses' heads."

Michelle laughed. "Castles moving and horses' heads jumping over people? You're sure this is a game for intellects?"

John paused. The long spoon, filled with vanilla ice cream, hung in mid-air halfway between the glass and his mouth. No one had ever before hinted that he might be intelligent. After all, his current grades were mostly "Bs" and "Cs," his mom still thought he was failing math, and the classics he most enjoyed were "Classics Illustrated" comic books.

"You have to be smart to play it," John heard himself say. The ice cream slowly slid from the spoon and plopped onto the counter.

"Careless boy."

John frowned and steadied the spoon to scoop up the rapidly melting mess. The next thing he knew, a hand came out of nowhere. It slapped down hard, sending the ice cream spraying in all directions. The largest lump landed squarely in John's face, the sticky substance smearing his glasses.

"Ha! Ha! Ha!"

John whipped off his glasses and stared at the offensive blur that was Petey O'Neal. He had stopped by Petersen's for his monthly issue of *Mad* and couldn't resist taunting the lovebirds. As usual, wherever Petey was, it was the wrong place at the wrong time.

"You jerk!" yelled John, jumping down from the stool.

Michelle grabbed his wrist. "Let it go," she pleaded.

"Yeah, do what she says, wimp. She wouldn't wanna see your face all beat up. Not that it looks all that great to begin with." Petey laughed at his own bad joke.

John found himself surprisingly under control. He realized it would be easy for him to ram his fist into Petey's lower jaw while the stupid boy was laughing, his head tilted backward.

With a little luck, the blow would crack a couple of teeth. Perhaps it was because he was with Michelle—a gentleman on a date with a beautiful young girl—that he didn't resort to brawling. Her words and firm touch had clearly comforted him during this sudden crisis. More likely, however, it was because John was beginning to comprehend who he was, and who he wasn't.

"Dry up, Petey," John said calmly. He turned his back on the boy and climbed up on the stool. He reached out for a napkin and, with one even stroke, wiped the streak of white off his glasses. He slid the frames back on and looked at Michelle. She nodded her quiet approval.

"Now," she said softly, "you were saying about the knights?"

The next sound John heard was the front door swinging open, accompanied by the jingle of its bell. A rush of cold air hit him in the back, but he never sensed it. Michelle was holding his hand.

***

If Petey found himself puzzled by the couple that day, the school was equally perplexed. They weren't, according to custom, going steady. They didn't sit together at lunch or dance together in the gym. John was never seen walking her to class, their books balanced together in his arms. And Michelle wore no outward symbol of their bond, no pendant or bracelet or ring. True, they had been seen at the movies and at Petersen's and, occasionally, talking in front of Michelle's locker. But no one had ever witnessed them holding hands or kissing in the hallways of Miller Junior High School.

In truth, John was happy with the way things were. At least for now. His parents didn't even know Michelle existed, and he hadn't confided much in Jeff since the day he'd told him off in the cafeteria. He was content to eat with Jeff, laugh at his lampoons of others, and assist him with his woodshop projects. But John often found himself tuning out the tall boy's chatter, opting instead to glance across the room at the girl who was rapidly changing his life for the better. He wasn't used to being in love, however, and he needed time to be alone with his feelings in order to sort them out.

These emotions most often manifested themselves as John tried to fall asleep at night. Art Roberts always began his 10:00 program on WLS with the three most-requested songs, culled from call-ins during the past few hours. As soon as these were aired, John switched off his transistor radio, set it on his nightstand, and arranged himself comfortably on his back, hands folded neatly across his chest. There, in the magnificent solitude of his darkened bedroom, staring out the open drapes at the bright stars of winter, he focused his thoughts on his future. A future with Michelle.

It was a simple future. A naïve future. They would marry, have children, and live in the suburbs. They would imitate his parents' relationship, only with more passion. They would hold hands, like in the Beatles song. They would kiss. They would live happily ever after.

Lying in bed, it didn't matter that these thoughts were a tad premature. He seldom dwelled on the fact that he had yet to kiss her. The quick peck on the cheek the night of their first date did not count. After all, it had been initiated solely and spontaneously by her. And he had barely felt it, his face being frozen at the time.

Soon, he supposed, he would get around to it. Soon, he imagined, he would lean in and kiss her full on the mouth, like he had seen Richard Beymer kiss Natalie Wood in *West Side Story*. Then, after the first time, a million other kisses would follow, sending him on a journey through space and time. And then . . .

The next thought startled him. He saw suddenly, like an unwanted intrusion, the face of Bill Dobbs. A conspiratorial look enveloped it as it inched closer. It spread its lips in a lascivious grin and spoke. "After you kiss 'em, the next step is second base. You know what that is, don't you, Belson? Don't be afraid. Girls love it when you feel 'em there. Then comes third base. That's a little tougher, but you'll get there someday. You'll see."

John started from the nightmare. He jumped out of bed and hurried to the bathroom. There, he gargled with Listerine to wash the taste of Bill Dobbs' sordid advice out of his nerve-wracked system.

16

"These are the forms for the eighth-grade field trip on April 15th." Mr. Schwartz held the papers aloft for all to see and then began to pass them out. "We will be going to the Museum of Science and Industry."

A bolt of energy shot through the classroom.

"Mrs. Danforth's homeroom will be joining us. The science teachers will also be coming along. We will be taking school buses for our transportation and purchasing sack lunches at the museum. Your parents must sign the permission forms as soon as possible." He glowered at the class in a way that suggested he thought this whole idea was a bad one. "That's as soon as possible, okay? And if any of your parents want to chaperone, ask them to give me a call."

Right, thought John, and every other kid in class thought likewise. No one was going to encourage a mom to come along so she could embarrass her child in front of teachers and peers.

"Now, please take out your history books," said Mr. Schwartz.

John was thrilled. He especially loved the museum's giant train layout. Whenever his parents had taken him, he'd wanted to circle around it all day. He would become paralyzed with rapture as he watched the trains crisscross the country, traversing steel bridges or appearing suddenly from the mouths of mountain tunnels. Once, the exhibit had been closed down for repairs, and John had moved quietly along in a sullen daze, not seeing or hearing or caring much about the other wonders of science and technology.

***

In general conversation during the day, John was surprised to learn that many of his classmates, including Jeff and Michelle, had never been to this museum. He praised it to Jeff at lunch.

"You'll like it. It's cool," John said between mouthfuls.

"What's there?" asked Jeff.

"A giant train layout. The biggest one you've ever seen."

Jeff shrugged. "So what?"

John was clearly speaking to a nonbeliever, but one who might yet be converted. "You'll see."

"What else is there?"

"Lots of stuff. There's a coal mine, and there's also a place where you can see yourself on TV. Oh, and there's a captured German submarine from World War II that you can walk through."

"A real German sub? Are you shittin' me?"

"Scout's honor."

"Well, that's more like it. What else?"

"Babies in a bottle."

"Huh?"

"There's a row of babies who died or something before they were born. And each one is at a different stage, like one month, two months, up to nine months. It's so you can see how babies develop inside their mothers."

"And they're all in one bottle?"

"No, dummy. Each one is in its own bottle."

"Weird."

"Yeah, but mostly sad. You know, 'cause they never got the chance to be born. They just sit there, preserved like the pig embryos in Mr. Schneider's classroom, waiting to be born. I guess their souls are with God."

"Or maybe in Limbo," Jeff ventured.

John suddenly thought about his relationship with Michelle. "Any other spooky stuff?"

John hesitated. "No, not really." He did not mention how he was still terrified to go inside Paul Bunyan's cabin. He had done it only once, as a six-year-old child, and had stumbled, screaming, back out the door, the vision of the giant man's bulging eyes and grinning row of teeth seared permanently into his brain. True, the woodsman wasn't as scary as the ancient mummies in the basement of the Field Museum. (As a youngster, John had pictured them coming alive like Boris Karloff.) But for an inanimate object, old Paul was pretty damn surreal.

***

During the next week, signed field trip forms were turned in. When asked about chaperones by his mom, John lied and said no more were needed. Mild trauma was produced when Mr. Schwartz explained that Mrs. Danforth's students would take a different bus and be split up into their own groups, meaning John and Michelle would not see each other all day, except perhaps at lunch. John had secretly hoped they would somehow end up in the same group, touring the various exhibits together, surreptitiously linking hands as they dove down the elevator shaft to the darkness of the coal mine or posing together for the TV cameras as a couple might for a wedding portrait. There was, however, one piece of news that, although bewildering, brightened John's day. In what was most likely a reflection of the stress Mr. Schwartz was feeling over the upcoming responsibility placed upon him, he had absent-mindedly put John and Jeff together in the same group, to be chaperoned by Donnie Johnson's neurotic, chain-smoking mother.

The bus ride to the museum was not without incident. Everyone was loaded on peaceably enough, and Mr. Schwartz checked and double-checked the roll. But no sooner did the driver maneuver the excited students out of the parking lot than Donnie Johnson spoke up loudly. "Mr. Schwartz, my mom's not on the bus!"

Knowing that she was going to have to go without smoking for the long trip, Mrs. Johnson had slipped out behind the building where the garbage dumpsters sat to inhale deeply from a menthol cigarette, already her third of the morning. Upon hearing the buses pulling out, she had dashed at full speed down the corridor and through the main lobby. She was just coming out into the gradually warming spring air when the buses pulled back into the lot.

"Hey, Donnie," asked Jeff, "was your mom sneakin' a 'rette?"

"Yeah," said Donnie, only slightly embarrassed. "She can't go too long without one."

Jeff filed this fact away for later.

The second incident came about when Bert Morris, bouncing happily along in the back of the bus and singing "Ninety-Nine Bottles of Beer on the Wall" with his friends, abruptly threw up. It didn't take long for the bad news—or the bad smell—to reach Mr. Schwartz up front. The driver, cursing under his breath, pulled off the expressway, followed by the other bus. At the first gas station, the students were unloaded, and the mess was cleaned up. Mr. Schwartz's biggest fear during the layover was that, separated from the group in the station's lot, some kid would simply wander off. It didn't happen, but Mrs. Johnson did need to use the restroom. Jeff nudged John, who saw the trail of smoke curling out through the transom above the door.

The majestic buildings that formed Chicago's skyline popped up shortly after the buses resumed their route. Faces pressed against the windows to stare out at them. Soon, the mini-caravan was through downtown and heading south on Lake Shore Drive. The sun's rays glinted off the whitecaps of Lake Michigan.

"Man, this is a long trip," moaned Jeff.

"Yeah, by the time we get there, we'll almost be in Indiana."

"What?"

"It's true. See where the shoreline curves up ahead? That's the bottom of the lake. Beyond that is Indiana."

This was the first time the two boys, sitting side by side, had spoken to each other since the unplanned stop. Jeff, seated closest to the window, had been content to look at the scenery. And John had thought of nothing but Michelle.

What was she doing on the other bus? Was anyone sitting with her, talking to her? Would he even see her at the museum? He had glimpsed her briefly at the gas station. Some of Mrs. Danforth's kids had lowered windows to ask what had happened on Mr. Schwartz's bus. Michelle had stuck her head out and smiled in his direction. He liked that. He liked that she wasn't some ditzy, flirty girl who would flip her hair back and throw him a kiss while all the kids and teachers and chaperones and bus drivers and gas station attendants stared at her. Or at him. He envied her calm composure regardless of whatever lunacy was swirling around her.

John's stomach rumbled. He hoped he wouldn't get sick like Bert. He neither needed nor wanted that kind of attention.

"We're here!" Mr. Schwartz's voice piped up above the din.

John shifted his gaze toward his teacher, who looked at that moment much like a man with a splitting headache. John reminded himself to never pursue this line of work.

"This is it?" asked Jeff. "It doesn't look like much."

John, weary of his friend's negativity, shot back, "Neither does your face."

"Ooooooh."

John rolled his eyes. "It's old. It was built in 1892 for a World's Fair called the Columbian Exposition. It's the only building that wasn't torn down afterward. That's why it doesn't look like much." The last line was delivered with sarcasm, the most frequent tone used lately when John was speaking to Jeff.

"Now, when you get off the bus," Mr. Schwartz was saying, "make sure you locate your chaperone immediately."

Sure, thought John, assuming she wasn't still on the bus, crouched down between the seats and puffing away.

Once inside the entryway, John spotted Michelle and tried to catch her eye, but she was looking around in amazement. John knew that, with her intellectual curiosity, she would love this place; he only wished he could take her by the hand to show her around.

"Now, stay with me and don't get lost," lectured Mrs. Johnson in a raspy voice as the groups headed off in different directions.

Her group of five consisted of John, Jeff, Donnie, and two nice girls, Janet Kolm and John's yearlong desk mate Susan Considine. All in all, it was a good mix, and it seemed unlikely there would be trouble. Donnie would have to obey his mother; John had turned over a new leaf; Jeff wouldn't take off without John; and the two girls wouldn't think about misbehaving until they were adults, and by then it would be too late.

The trains occupied everyone's attention for a good half hour. Even Jeff, the skeptic, was impressed. And, as Mrs. Johnson watched the thin bursts of white smoke belch forth from the passing steam engines, she twitched.

"Did you see her back there?" said Jeff as they moved on.

"Who?"

"Mrs. Johnson. She's having withdrawal. Mark my words: she'll ditch us soon, and then we can take off."

"Oh, grow up."

***

"That sub was really cool," Jeff admitted as they headed off to lunch. In the stuffy basement cafeteria, the two eighth-grade groups came together. They crowded into picnic tables, their sack lunches handed out by their teachers. No one sat next to Bert Morris.

John and Jeff found a spot at the end of one of the long, graffiti-marred tables and sat down facing each other. They examined their identical lunches, prepared ahead of time by the museum's cafeteria ladies. Each sack contained a ham and cheese sandwich covered in Miracle Whip with an apple and a small bag of Fritos. To drink was the requisite carton of milk.

"Well, at least it's not olive loaf," sneered Jeff as he bit into the dry bread.

"Mind if I sit here?"

Hallelujah, thought John. "Please do."

Michelle slid her legs one at a time over the bench seat.

John momentarily lost his breath.

"So, are you boys enjoying the museum?"

"It's okay," said Jeff before John could answer. "I guess it's better than I thought it would be."

"What have you seen so far?"

John fed back the morning's itinerary.

"Wait until you see the coal mine," said Michelle. "It's fascinating. And we went inside a human heart to see how it works. I've learned so much today. Oh, and we went inside Paul Bunyan's cabin. He was a giant, like in the legend. It made me laugh."

John cringed.

"We're hoping Mrs. Johnson sneaks off for a smoke," said Jeff. "Then we can head out on our own."

John stared blankly in Jeff's direction. "And with our luck, we'll probably get lost in the mine and end up being buried alive when a tunnel collapses."

Michelle smiled. "That sounds like par for you two."

"Yeah," Jeff conceded, "and Mr. Schwartz will probably be happy when he finds out we're dead."

"How can you even say a thing like that?" demanded Michelle. "You know everyone would miss you terribly if you were gone."

"No, they wouldn't," Jeff snorted contemptuously. "Wake up and smell the roses, bright eyes. If anyone should know that, it's you. I mean, do any of your classmates from your old school ever write to you? You know, just to say 'hello'? Mine sure as hell don't. That's because we were never anything other than a diversion for them. 'Oh, look, there's the boy who's always getting into trouble, and there's that girl who sits by herself at lunch and reads. What a couple of losers.' They label us; we accept it and behave the way we're supposed to. In the end, they hate us 'cause we're different, 'cause we don't fit in. So, if we move away or even die, nobody cares. And the kids who show up at the funeral and cry are doing it just for show—the worst kind of phonies."

John sat silent, stunned by the outburst.

Michelle's eyes were rimmed with tears.

"Look, I'm sorry," said Jeff, reaching his hand out to touch Michelle's. "I didn't mean to upset you. I'm sure you're right. We'd be missed."

With that, the tall boy stood, gathered up his half-eaten lunch, and excused himself. "You two probably want to be alone, so I'll go see what Donnie Johnson's up to."

Silence hung in the air like rain clouds.

"Are you okay?" ventured John.

"I'm fine," answered Michelle, wiping away a lone tear.

"I don't know what got into him."

"It's all right. Can we walk?"

They walked out a far door, each step taking them further from the clamor of the cafeteria.

"Do you ever think about it, John?"

"About what?"

"About dying. About where you'll go when you die, and about the people you'll leave behind. I know my mom would miss me. She doesn't have anybody else. As for them,"—Michelle gestured to the crowd behind her—"we just have to be ourselves and hope that others accept us for who we are."

They reached a stairwell and climbed to the first landing. The main floor with its train layout was directly above them. But they were alone.

John turned to face Michelle. His hands, trembling, reached out to take hold of her shoulders. "I know what I think. I think it doesn't matter about those other kids. Not since I met you." The words were racing out now, like a fast-moving train gliding along silver tracks. "I think you're the nicest, prettiest girl I've ever known, and I don't want you to hurt anymore."

He leaned in and kissed her. The kiss itself was neither too short nor too long. The warmth of Michelle's lips flooded through his body as if he'd inhaled Vicks, and when he broke away, her gentle eyes smiled up at him.

John had envisioned this moment since the first day he had seen her walk into the girls' gym after lunch. But, of all the places he had dreamed it would happen—after school at her locker, inside the movie theatre, on her front steps as he dropped her off from an ice cream date—he'd never imagined it would take place in a grimy, dim stairwell at the Museum of Science and Industry.

As they walked back to the cafeteria, they held hands. Michelle seemed content. And John was pleasantly surprised that he had found something at the museum that he liked better than the trains.

17

When John and Michelle danced together after lunch in the girls' gym the very next day, it became official. They were a couple, and the entire school took notice. Susan Considine told John she was happy for him because Michelle seemed like an intelligent girl. Gail Swanson surprised him by stopping by his locker to say the two would be good for each other. And, passing him in the hall, Bill Dobbs just smiled and clutched his crotch.

It had been sealed with that first kiss the day before in the museum stairwell. It was a time and place John would remember forever, a milestone in his life that thrust him forward into the next phase of his adolescence. Ironically, another benchmark of sorts occurred just a few days later. This one, however, brought John considerably less pleasure.

***

"We can take the train," said Michelle. She was seated next to John at the boys' lunch table, another visible signpost to the world that they were boyfriend and girlfriend. Jeff, seated across from them, didn't seem to mind. After all, he was still the school's iconoclast, and he would sit where and with whom he damn well pleased.

"It won't cost much," Michelle continued, "and we can do anything we want."

Ever since the field trip, Michelle had displayed a Carl Sandburg-like obsession with the city. The mere thought of running free through its maze of sidewalks and parks, hemmed in by towering buildings and seductive storefront windows, had throttled her ability to think of anything else. She was, in psychological terms, a goner.

"I think it would be great fun," Jeff chimed in. "You should take her."

"Maybe . . ."

John's hesitancy was well founded. Although his new love assumed that he was familiar with the city, the truth was that John knew very little about the rather large and frightening place. He had grown up in the sheltered suburbs, and other than an occasional trip with his parents to shop at Marshall Field's during the Christmas season, he never ventured downtown. Now, however, Michelle was batting her eyelashes and smiling that wickedly delicious smile in John's direction, and his resolve was melting faster than a cheap candle.

"Well, if you don't want to go, I'll understand." Perfectly planned pause. "Maybe Jeff would like to take me."

Jeff looked up from his Jell-O pudding, taken aback for a half second. "Sure, I'll go."

Inwardly, John heaved a sigh of relief. Normally, he would have preferred to be alone with Michelle, but Jeff would make the perfect third wheel. Friend on one hand, bodyguard on the other. If some city thug tried to mug them in an alleyway, the tall, tough boy, unafraid of anyone, would fight him off while John and Michelle ran for help. Yes, this arrangement would work nicely.

"Okay, I'm in."

"Great!" yelled Michelle, reaching over to hug John around his neck. "I've got the train schedule right here in my purse."

As Michelle outlined the plan—meet at the station at 8:30 and buy round-trip tickets, depart at 8:40, arrive at 9:30—John drifted away. Growing up, much of what he had read or watched on TV had been classified as adventure. "The Adventures of Robin Hood." "The Adventures of the Hardy Boys." And now he was going on his own adventure. Not a safe, school-sponsored event with chaperones or a carefully supervised outing to a Cubs game with his parents, but a real-life, down-and-dirty, free-as-the-wind journey into the urban unknown.

A rush of excitement surged suddenly through John's body. He was exhilarated by the thrill of mingling with strange men and women who wore wide-brimmed hats and wraparound scarves to conceal their identities; by the lure of walking on cold concrete stained with gum and mustard; by the feel of menacing skyscrapers closing in around them like ancient sentries guarding their temples; by the—

"John, are you okay?" Michelle's voice broke into his danger-driven delirium. "Your face is flush."

John put his hands to his cheeks and felt the burning sensation. Embarrassed, he turned even redder. "Yeah, fine. It's just hot in here, that's all."

Jeff grinned at him across the table. "Why don't you get a drink of water to calm your nerves?"

John frowned. "Number one, I'm not thirsty. Number two, I'm not nervous—about anything."

"Suit yourself."

John felt Michelle's hand settling upon his. "Let's not worry. When we're downtown, we'll stick together. If we watch out for one another, nothing bad will happen."

Jeff reached over and ceremoniously placed his hand atop the others. "To nothing bad."

***

The train, moving slowly, slid out of the sunshine and into the blackness of the multi-track station. The three friends pressed their faces against the green-tinted windows and stared out at the stark scene. Dimly lit and uninviting, the cavernous building seemed almost empty, save for one lonely train sitting several tracks beyond theirs. Had they pulled in on a weekday morning, they would have been startled to see the endless stream of men wearing dark business suits and polished shoes—all of them carrying trim briefcases that swung in rhythm to their measured steps—rushing past them toward yet another day of work. Achingly, with wheels squeaking loudly, the train crawled to a stop.

John, Jeff, and Michelle disembarked. They strolled through the depot—past the little shop selling tobacco and magazines, the shoeshine stand with its incredibly efficient laborers, and the honor boxes shouting out the day's headlines from their glass fronts. Every nuance of the strange place caught their curiosity. When they finally walked through the doors and stepped onto the shaded sidewalk, a blast of cold wind nearly knocked them to the pavement.

"Ha!" laughed Jeff. "No wonder they call this the Windy City."

"Actually," John corrected, "that's because of the loud-mouthed politicians."

"What? You're kiddin', right?"

"No, it's true," said Michelle, who had been devouring reading material on Chicago for the last few days.

"So, where shall we go first?" asked John, looking at Michelle.

"Let's go to State Street and visit Field's!"

Somewhat reluctantly, the boys agreed. "But not for long," said Jeff.

The promise of a gorgeous spring Saturday hung in the chill morning air. The sun continued its ascent, and the wind seemed to be dying down—at least a little—as the threesome headed out on their journey. Michelle was ecstatic. She zigzagged her way around people, always eager to see what came next. Movie theatres, restaurants, and hotels were spaced out among stores selling exclusive products such as books, candy, shoes, and men's suits. Drug stores featured not only soda fountain treats but lunch counter meals as well. At one point, the boys, straining to keep pace, turned a corner only to discern that Michelle was nowhere in sight.

"Oh, no," wailed John. "Where is she? I thought we were going to stick together."

"There she is," said Jeff. He pointed toward the window of a small shop through which they saw a smiling Michelle waving at them.

They pushed through the glass door to the tinkling sound of a bell and the sweet smell of a mix of popcorn flavors.

"I thought we were supposed to stay together," chastised John, clearly shaken at the thought of losing Michelle.

"I knew where you were."

"But we didn't know where you were."

"I was in here."

"So I see."

Michelle was already digging around in her purse. "We have to buy some popcorn."

No argument there, thought the boys. Deciding on the best of all worlds, they each purchased a bag of their own but of a different kind so they could share. John bought regular; Michelle, caramel; Jeff, cheese. All were hot and fresh and tasted better than any popcorn they had ever eaten in their entire lives. John began to appreciate the big city a little more with every mouthful. An El train rumbled noisily overhead.

The rest of the morning was spent riding the escalators—another first for Michelle—up and down the floors of Field's, searching out the giant department store's many displays. A pair of white spring gloves grabbed Michelle's attention, tempting John to buy them for her until he saw the price tag. He had set aside a few dollars to buy lunch for her; that was all he could afford.

"I'm hungry," said Jeff. "Let's find someplace to eat."

"These are beautiful," said Michelle, ignoring him as she fondled the gloves. "I wish I could afford them."

"Well, you can't. So, let's eat."

Pouting, she carefully set them down.

John spoke up. "I've got a great idea for lunch. Why don't we find a street vendor and buy hot dogs?"

"Sounds good to me," said Jeff.

"Michelle?"

"Okay, sounds like fun."

In fact, this was exactly the type of experience Michelle wanted. Nothing spoke Chicago more than its kosher dogs.

Ten minutes and one helpful traffic cop later, they were ordering their meal from a heavyset, balding man who somehow reminded John of his Uncle Tony. The professional, using metal tongs, pinched the slender pieces of meat between the sides of the poppy seed buns. Then, like a master painter, he slapped on the mustard and relish, scooped on the tomatoes and onions, placed a dill pickle neatly alongside each wiener, and showered them all with several shakes of celery salt.

Unwisely, Jeff asked, "Where's the ketchup?"

The businessman's genial expression turned sour. "Ketchup? Ketchup? I suppose you're one of those jokers who puts ketchup on his eggs. You want ketchup? Not on my dogs."

"Sorry," said John, stepping in to pinch-hit for his ignorant friend. "He doesn't know any better. He grew up in Iowa."

"Iowa? You put ketchup on your corn on the cob too?"

"What?" yelled an instantly angry Jeff. "Are you tellin' me nobody in this whole damn city ever put ketchup on one of these turds you're selling us?"

"Yeah, sonny, that's what I'm telling you. Unless you wanna ruin a perfectly good meal."

John and Michelle were now staring at each other. Perhaps it had not been such a splendid idea to bring Jeff along as a bodyguard after all. They had paid for the dogs before the man made them—he had insisted on this—and now they just wanted to grab the food and go.

"Listen, mister." John's voice was quivering now. He was afraid that a fight might break out any minute. How embarrassing would *that* be? It was one thing to be knifed or clubbed by gangland hoods, but to be beaten with tongs? "Could we just have our hot dogs, please?"

John, sweating, locked eyes with Jeff, silently pleading with him to control his temper and not make an even bigger scene.

Already, a crowd of curious gapers had paused to watch the heated exchange. For a few suspenseful seconds, no one said a word. Then, without hesitation, the vendor deftly wrapped the three Chicago-style hot dogs in tissue, grasped them all in one hairy hand, and passed them across to John.

"Hope your friend enjoys his first real dog."

John, Jeff, and Michelle moved rapidly away from the corner stand. They ate as they walked.

Michelle savored her first bite. "Mmmm, this is really good."

"I told you you'd love it," said John, now looking at Jeff to gauge his first reaction.

"You were right. This tastes great. I guess Mr. Friendly is a world-class chef after all."

The storm cloud passed, and the three friends suddenly found themselves in bright sunlight on Michigan Avenue.

"That's Grant Park." John pointed to the other side of the busy street. "And that's Lake Michigan beyond it."

Michelle had her heart set on the lake.

They crossed at a light and hurried swiftly through the gorgeous park, only pausing when John, pointing north, commanded them to look up. "That's the Prudential Building. It's the tallest skyscraper in the city."

"Oh, it's all so thrilling," exclaimed Michelle in response. She spun around in a joyful circle, arms spread out to her sides. Suddenly, in the devil-may-care attitude that so perfectly underscored her approach to life, she took off running toward the vast expanse of blue-grey water stretching out to the distant horizon.

"C'mon! Catch me if you can!"

"Wait," said Jeff, reaching out and grabbing the tail end of John's jacket. "Let's give her a big lead and then blow past her."

"Let me go," said John, brushing Jeff's hand away. And he took off running in pursuit.

Perhaps he should not have been so eager; perhaps he should have listened to his friend. But when you're young and in love for the first time in your life . . . well, that explains everything.

He almost caught her as she fled through the lush landscape on the crisscrossing concrete pathways. Her laughter, caught by the wind, carried back to him. At that very moment, John Belson was happier than he had ever been in his life.

He never even saw the bicycle.

18

When John awoke, he was surprised to find himself comfortably stretched out on a hospital bed. He was even more surprised to find his left foot in a cast, and he took note of the fact that his head throbbed and his vision was blurred. He turned his head gently to the left and noticed a nurse reading a chart. He groaned, and the woman in white smiled at him.

"What happened?" he croaked. His throat felt like sandpaper.

"Here, drink this," she said, handing him a Dixie Cup filled with water.

He held the cup with shaky hands and drank. The cool liquid slid down his parched throat.

"I'll be right back." The nurse, leaving her patient alone with his confused thoughts, went out into the brightly lit hallway. From a distance, John heard her say, "He's awake. You can see him now."

His parents were shown into the room. Stress lined their faces, but they brightened when they saw their son. It was explained to John that he had suffered a broken ankle and a concussion, but his parents seemed to know little else. Since John remembered nothing, Jeff and Michelle were summoned from the waiting room down the hall.

Michelle's tear-stained face was first through the door. She cautiously approached the bed.

John was thrilled to see her. Remembering his manners, he turned to his parents and slurred, "Mom, Dad, this is my girlfriend. Her name is Michelle Watson."

As if John's folks hadn't had enough shock for one day.

"Oh," said Mrs. Belson. And then, after scrutinizing Michelle, added, "It's very nice to meet you."

John's dad nodded perfunctorily in her direction and then blurted out, "What have you done to my son?"

"I can answer that," said Jeff. "I told the ambulance guys and the doctors everything before you arrived. This is what happened."

Michelle drew a breath and held it.

"We were running through the park, all of us together." Jeff glanced furtively at Michelle. "But, as you probably know, Mrs. Belson, John's quite the athlete, and he pulled ahead of the two of us."

Suddenly proud as she pictured the race, John's mom smiled.

"So, as I was saying, John was in the lead when all of a sudden this crazy bicyclist came racing out of nowhere and slammed into him."

Mrs. Belson winced.

"As you know, John's as tough as nails. I honestly believe he wouldn't have been hurt if this guy had just fallen off to the side when his bike went down. But, no. He flew up and over the handlebars and came crashing down on top of John."

Jeff paused for effect.

"And did I tell you what this clown looked like? Well, for starters, he must have weighed at least three hundred pounds. Can you just picture poor Johnny standing there looking up while the sky went dark and this blimp came down like the Hindenburg on top of him? When Fatso landed, John's foot got caught up under him. That's when I heard the bone crack."

Mrs. Belson winced again.

"Then, I heard his head hit the pavement. I rolled Lardman off him and asked him what hurt. He didn't answer. By then, adults were everywhere, and someone ran off to find a phone and call for help."

Doubtful, John's father prodded Jeff. "Didn't the bicycle have the right of way?"

"I think what's most important is that your son will recover from what could have been an even more serious accident." The voice belonged to a doctor who had been standing silently just inside the doorway listening to Jeff's mostly truthful story. "And, by the way, I'm sure you'll be happy to hear that the bicycle rider, a Mr. Lanzen"—here he stopped momentarily and stared at Jeff—"was not hurt. He told me to wish the young man good luck in his recovery."

John soaked all of this in as best he could. His head still ached, and he felt drowsy as well. So that was what had happened? He couldn't remember seeing the bicycle approach him, couldn't remember the moment of impact. What he *could* visualize was the image of a beautiful girl—Michelle?—running away from him. And, like in a dream, his languid pursuit was somehow drawing him ever closer to her. Ever closer. Closer.

He looked up and saw Michelle. Tears were weaving their way down her ashen cheeks. She looked into his eyes and whispered, "I'm sorry." She then turned her head and looked at Jeff. John couldn't be sure, but he thought she mouthed the words, "Thank you."

Meanwhile, the doctor's distant voice was saying to his parents, "We'll have you fill out a few forms, we'll rent you some crutches, and then you can take him home."

***

John Belson was miserable. The month of May in the Midwest was normally the first—and only—month of genuine spring, which meant warmer days and later sunsets. The bright green lushness of young buds in bloom spawned dreams of just-around-the-corner summer. More than anything, it meant for John the return of baseball.

And with his foot propped on the living room sofa, staring out the window at the antics of two squirrels chasing each other up and down the parkway's giant elm trees, John felt its loss and regretted it deeply. Bill Dobbs, in the nicest way possible, had told John that his iron glove would be missed at third base and that, when the chips were down, they'd win one for him. But that was hollow consolation, especially since this was to have most likely been his last year of organized ball. Next year would come tryouts for the high school team, and unless his skills improved dramatically by then, John knew it would prove a futile exercise.

Michelle did her best to keep him from feeling sorry for himself. She would walk over after dinner and play chess with him in the fresh, cool air of the outdoor patio, their concentration broken only by the distant barking of dogs and the tinkling bells of the Good Humor truck making its way slowly up the suburban street.

"Do you want an ice cream?" Michelle asked. "Oh, by the way, check."

John frowned. He dug into his jeans pocket and pulled out two quarters. "I'll take a Toasted Almond Bar. Get what you want. By the time you run out there and back, I'll have gotten myself out of this mess."

"Yeah," Michelle teased, "probably by moving several pieces around."

She ran toward the street, waving down the driver.

Seeing her run, John sulked. He reflected on the fact that, had he been alone, the ice cream man would have been long gone by the time he braced himself on his crutches and hobbled out to the street. He didn't like relying on Michelle. He didn't like relying on anyone. At least his parents had come to know—and accept—Michelle. This, he thought, was one positive result of the accident. The other good thing was that there were no lingering effects from the concussion. The few mild headaches he had suffered during the first several days had gradually receded until he felt fine again.

John turned his attention back to the board. Michelle had snuck her queen into a diagonal line leading to his already beleaguered king. He sensed the battle wouldn't last much longer. He had taught her well, and she was a quick learner. He contemplated cheating, remembered it was a game of honor, and emitted a weary sigh. He moved his king one space, boxing the monarch in even more.

"Ooooh, you look so serious. Here's your Toasted Almond." She held a Chocolate Éclair Bar in her other hand.

The treat cheered John up. For a short time.

"I've been giving some thought to the eighth-grade dance."

John rolled his eyes. Suddenly, the ice cream didn't taste as good.

"Have you thought about it? I mean, you're not going to miss it, are you?"

Of course John had thought about it. He had dwelled and brooded on it until he could barely think. This end-of-the-school-year ritual was as important as graduation, more so to the students. Why else had John allowed his parents to sign him up for Cotillion during the past winter?

Common in this era, this organization taught teens the proper behavior and correct dance steps for any social occasion. The ballroom dances that were taught included the box step, the fox trot, the waltz, and—for those wild moments—the cha-cha.

John's teachers had been a stern husband-and-wife team who frowned upon teens in general and boys in particular. Consequently, John had attended these lessons—held every Tuesday night in a small grammar school gym in which the temperature never fell below a balmy 102 degrees—with very little enthusiasm. The heat, along with the anxiety created by pairing up with some very attractive girls, had caused John to perspire profusely. Forced to "move to the left and greet the young lady with a handshake," John had often caught a quick look of disgust in his dance partner's eyes upon coming in touch with his sweaty palm.

He had, however, determinedly gutted it out. And now—irony of all ironies—John was in love with a real-live girl who loved him back, the formal dance was a week away, and he was as crippled as Tiny Tim.

"Well?"

"Well what?"

"Are you going to the dance? We get our bid books tomorrow." She smiled seductively at her overmatched opponent as she took the final bite of her bar, sliding the melting ice cream off the stick and into her mouth. "I'd hate to see it get filled while you're trying to make up your mind."

"Oh, great. Let me get this straight. I get to go to the dance just so I can lean against a wall and watch you twist the night away with every boy in our class. Why doesn't that sound like a good idea to me?"

"Don't be silly. You can dance . . . the slow ones anyway."

That much was true. John could probably box step the romantic dances while leaning on Michelle, not a terribly repulsive thought. But the crutches would make the rest of the night awkward, if not difficult. Certainly not the way John had pictured it only weeks earlier after their first kiss.

The realization that he had not kissed her since that day in the museum stairwell came up in his throat. He had assumed they would have plenty of time alone to take spring walks through verdant fields until they tumbled casually to the grass in each other's arms for an extended kiss-a-thon. But the damn crutches kept him at home in the evenings—under the intrusive glare of his annoying parents. What was he supposed to do? Knock over the chessboard, jump across the table, pull Michelle to him, and start making out? As soon as he got up the nerve to do it, the screen door would squeak open to reveal his apron-clad mother, who would cheerfully shout out, "Would you kids care for some lemonade?"

"John, what's wrong?"

"Nothing." He paused. "Everything."

"Don't you trust me?"

"More than anybody in the world."

"Good. Then I promise we'll have a wonderful time at the dance. I know you feel bad about missing the baseball season and not being a hundred percent for all of the end-of-the-year fun, but it'll be okay. You've got to believe me."

John looked into her eyes. "I believe you."

She smiled. "Then that's settled."

"Yeah."

She rose. "I have to be getting home now. My mom will think we eloped. I'll see you tomorrow."

"See ya," said John, a contented look now on his face.

"Oh," she said, "one more thing." She stretched her fingers down and carefully placed one of her knights in its new position on the chessboard. "Checkmate."

19

When the sixteen-inch softball shot up off the ground and caught Jeff Womack squarely in the groin, John Belson laughed out loud. Of course, there was nothing funny about it. But, lately, his inactivity had caused a mean streak to show itself. This time it unveiled itself due to jealousy. The other boys were in their gym clothes (blue shorts and white T-shirts with last names in Mom-print across the front) having fun in the mid-morning sun while John sat in street clothes staring with envy from his seat on the metal bleachers, his ever-present crutches by his side.

A pinch of guilt pricked him as he watched Jeff roll around in the diamond dirt, a portrait of genuine pain. Several boys, hands on their knees, stood leaning over the writhing boy, looks of sympathy etched on their faces. Mr. Dumpmore, who had been umpiring the balls and strikes from a relatively safe spot behind the pitcher, was the first to speak.

"Does it hurt?"

Jeff responded with an agonizing groan.

"It hurts, huh? Well, you better sit this one out. Boys, help him to the sidelines, will ya?"

Hunched over, Jeff walked gingerly off the playing field, assisted on either side by guys who were just thankful it hadn't happened to them. They eased the tall boy down into the soft grass and returned to the game.

Jeff rested on his back, knees up, and took a series of deep breaths. The last one seemed, finally, to push out the pain.

"Out with the bad air, huh?" asked John, who had worked his way from the bleachers to Jeff's side.

Jeff nodded, still unable—or unwilling—to speak.

"Sorry," said John, hoping that Jeff had not heard him laugh.

"Was that you laughing?"

"No," John lied. "I think it was Dumpmore."

Jeff shielded his eyes from the sun, searching John's silhouette for the truth. "I suppose it *was* pretty damn funny to watch."

John grinned and sat down beside his friend.

After a short time, Jeff pushed himself up on one elbow. He reached between his legs and gently caressed the wounded area.

"That can't feel good."

"It definitely does not. I hope this doesn't hamper my dance moves on Saturday night."

"Well, if it does, you and I can sit in the corner like a couple of rejects and watch everyone else have a good time."

Self-pity, never far away, was creeping into John's psyche again.

"Now, now. Don't feel sorry for yourself. You know as well as I that the lovely maiden Michelle will not allow that to happen. She'll brush off the other guys like dead flies and come sit on your lap all night."

The image made John smile.

The two boys sat quietly for a time. John reflected on the past year—how lucky he'd been to find Jeff; how they'd hit it off so quickly; how they'd thrown ropes to each other when help was most needed. John was convinced their fallouts were behind them, that the next four years in high school would only see their friendship grow.

"By the way, I've been meaning to tell you something." Jeff's voice sounded somehow unsure, as if he didn't want to continue. An errant cloud briefly blocked the sun. "My parents told me a couple nights ago. They're sending me to St. Sebastian's in the fall."

John felt like he was drowning. He lifted his head to see the life preserver, beyond his desperate reach, bobbing away from him across the turbulent ocean.

"What?"

"Yeah. That blows, huh? They want me to get a Catholic education, so no more public schools for me. I think they want me to become a priest. Can you imagine?"

Imagine what? thought John. A giant wave slid over his head, pulling him down where he could no longer breathe. Imagine walking through the yawning doors of the gothic-like high school this fall and *not* seeing his best friend waving him toward four years of frenetic fun? Imagine drifting apart through space and time like a really scary "Twilight Zone" episode?

John buried his face in his hands and said nothing as his lungs slowly filled with water. He might as well drown with dignity.

"Sorry, man, it's not what I wanted either."

John remained slumped over and silent. The wandering cloud drifted on, allowing the sun to burn the back of his neck.

"Just think," continued Jeff in an attempt to resuscitate his friend. "If you start sinning with Michelle, I can hear your confession. And I promise to let you off with an easy penance."

John cocked his head slightly toward Jeff, who was grinning like the Cheshire Cat. Seconds earlier, near tears, John could not have thought of laughing. Now, presented with the vision of his friend clothed in priestly vestments while sitting in a confessional listening to people's darkest deeds, he could not keep it in.

Jeff, knowing his audience, poured it on. "Now, my son, tell me what you did with your girlfriend in the back seat of your daddy's car. Yes, that's right, go on. Don't spare any details, or I cannot absolve you from your sins."

Both boys laughed out loud. Pain suddenly seized Jeff again, and he stopped abruptly. "Owww."

"Hurts, huh? That'll teach you to make fun of the priesthood." In fact, John would mostly miss the way Jeff ridiculed anybody and anything; the more pompous or prestigious, the more likely a target.

The bell on the side of the building rang loudly, cutting into John's nostalgic thoughts about his fallen comrade.

"Help him up, will ya?" barked Mr. Dumpmore. "And get him into the building."

For a second, John wasn't sure which of them the fat man was addressing. But then, did it matter?

John stood first, balancing on a crutch. He leaned down, locked his forearm beneath Jeff's armpit, and hoisted him to his feet. Jeff then stretched down, picked up John's other crutch, and handed it to him. Together, they hobbled across the dandelion-covered expanse of spring grass. Not a word was spoken between them.

***

The last full week of school. A blur. Books were turned in; lockers were cleaned out. Mr. Schwartz lectured the class for a full hour on the importance of getting a good start in high school. This was their chance to put to use all they had learned at Miller Junior High. To show their new teachers that they had been given a strong foundation in the basic subjects. To spotlight their industriousness, their studiousness, their trustworthiness.

My Lord, thought John, were we going off to high school or war?

Mr. Schwartz wasn't finished. High school was serious business, and some people's idea of fun and games would simply not be tolerated. He glanced sharply at Jeff. Everyone knew by now where Jeff was headed, and John guessed that Mr. Schwartz was taunting the boy, letting him know that the strict Catholic disciplinarians were waiting to beat him down.

"A second chance, a new beginning, a clean slate." Mr. Schwartz stopped and smiled, not unkindly, at his students. "Good luck to you all."

"Bonne chance," added Miss Parras.

Next came the most celebrated of all end-of-school traditions, the passing out of yearbooks. For those last few days, kids who had never spoken to one another happily signed the annuals with fond farewells and overtures to "call me." Words of wisdom abounded. "I'm writing in your crack. How does it feel?" was a time-honored favorite. Jeff drew a caricature in John's book of Michelle fleeing from John as he panted after her on crutches. The balloon above him read, "I WUV YOU! MARRY ME AND MAKE BABIES WITH ME!" Michelle, meanwhile, was running toward Jeff's outstretched arms saying, "NO WAY! I WANT A REAL MAN!"

John, as usual, was moved to tears of laughter by Jeff's comical drawing. He made a mental note to show it to Michelle.

The absolute highlight of the week was the eighth-grade prank. Simply put, it was a doozy. In those days, suburbs and farmland bumped cozily up against each other, and it wasn't that difficult for fourteen-year-old boys to get their hands on piglets—or, for that matter, a can of grease. But the truly ingenious aspect of the ruse was the numbering system devised by the students in charge. Jeff, John, Bill Dobbs, and the others carefully spray-painted the stark white numbers 1, 2, and 4 on the sides of the three little pigs.

The cafeteria rocked with squeals, screams, and swear words as the teachers attempted to capture the slippery swine. Finally, Arvid the janitor, using more intelligence than anyone had ever credited him with, tempted the pigs with some of the school's lunch fare. He slopped it in a trail to the floor of his closet, watched them eagerly gulp it down, and simply shut the door behind them when they went in for more. Pleased with his resourcefulness, he slumped against the wall and said, "Da Lord made da man to rule over da beasts."

The game, of course, was not yet over. Lights burned brightly throughout the night at Miller Junior High School as a thoroughly spent and very angry Mr. Carver, assisted by most of the male teachers, searched high and low for piggy number 3. Every now and then, a profanity-laced tirade against the world in general—and eighth-grade smart-asses in particular—echoed out into the warm night air.

20

John Belson was no longer lonely. Why should he be? Although it was a major disappointment that Jeff's parents were sending him to St. Sebastian's, John was confident they would see each other often and remain fast friends. This was a lie, of course, and the passing of time would prove it to be so. But John didn't know this for sure yet, so it was probably best to stick with the self-deception. It would make it easier to play out the eighth-grade dance and graduation.

And besides, he reasoned as he fumbled with his tie, he had Michelle now, and that was enough. He slid the knot into place, took a handkerchief and patted the sweat beads on his forehead, and slipped on his matching navy blue sports coat. Grabbing his crutches, he hobbled out the back door. His parents, waiting in the driveway, drove him to the ball.

On this first weekend of June, the sun, beginning its descent, shone down on the beautiful dresses of the young ladies as they stepped out of the endless line of cars and strode awkwardly on high heels toward the school. Once inside, they were directed through the courtyard, which was adorned with early summer flowers.

Here, a hired photographer had set up his camera to snap posed pictures of the revelers with their friends. Some shots showed four or five girls, arms draped around one another, happy smiles beaming into the lens. A few framed a guy and a girl in a dreamy "we're in love" portrait. Technically, there were no dates. The administration had sent home notes asking parents to escort their young teens to and from the dance, and teachers helped all the girls fill their bid books so no one would feel left out. Ten dances, ten different dates. A good plan.

But, as John balanced himself and waited impatiently for Michelle to arrive, he wasn't so sure he was going to enjoy watching her dance with other boys. Boys like goofy Donnie Johnson, who had never danced with a girl and would probably drool all over her. Boys like lecherous Bill Dobbs, who would slowly slide his hand down her lower back toward her bottom. Boys like pathetic Petey O'Neal, who hadn't signed her bid book and who, if he even so much as approached her on the dance floor, would be beaten to a pulp by a crutches-wielding psychopath.

The blood-soaked image of Petey's disfigured body lying helplessly on the gym's hardwood floor was replaced by the vision of a gorgeous young girl in a Cinderella dress crossing the threshold of the courtyard door.

Wow, thought John. How had this ever happened to him?

Michelle's eyes met his, and his lips spread into a spontaneous smile. Tonight would be all right after all.

She approached him and took his hand. "Been waiting long?"

"An eternity. But it was worth it. You look fantastic."

"Why, thank you. You look rather charming yourself." She reached up and straightened his tie, a basic female instinct.

"Shall we have our picture taken?" John asked.

"Mais oui."

John took her arm and escorted her over to the line. Five minutes later, a short, smiling man who introduced himself as Mr. Drake straightened John's tie (again) and arranged the couple. John stood behind Michelle, his hands on her waist, a position John would not have dared on his own.

"Tilt your head, young man. Your glasses are reflecting the sunlight. This way; a little bit more; hold it! Now say, 'Sex.'"

The two giggled; the camera clicked.

"Okay, you're done. Come back for your free prints later this evening." The memorabilia, parting gifts to the eighth graders meant to capture this moment in time, were being paid for by the PTA.

"Jeez, what a pervert," laughed John as they walked toward the gym. "Why didn't he make us say 'cheese' like normal?"

"Because he wanted you to relax. He knew boys always tense up in formal situations."

"That's not true," said John defensively.

"Sure it is. Your hands were digging into my hips."

Rather than continue the argument-that-would-not-be-won, John changed the subject. "So, did you get that summer job at the park district yet?"

"Let's not talk about the summer. Let's just have fun tonight."

John thought it was an odd answer but said nothing in reply.

They entered the gym. It was decorated much like the winter ball several months earlier. Blue and white balloons—the school colors—hugged the rafters, bouncing along in helium-filled delight. Streamers of the same colors dipped down from above the entryway doors and along the sides of the walls. A large banner suspended from curtain to curtain above the stage at one end of the gym read: CONGRATULATIONS CLASS OF 1964!

Neat rows of bakery cookies rested in silver trays atop linen-covered tables. Next to these trays, two punch bowls contained rainbow sherbet in a ginger ale base.

Most thrilling of all was the live band that played beneath the banner, hammering out a mixture of fast and slow dance numbers, including almost unrecognizable covers of current Top 40 hits. The quintet (bass, rhythm guitar, lead guitar, organ, and drums) called their group The Water's Edge, a rather serene identity for a garage band from the local high school. The music, more than anything, gave cultural relevance to the dance, putting a teenage stamp of approval on it that past formals had not earned. This was not the Lawrence Welk or Guy Lombardo to which their parents moved; this was the harmony of *their* generation. And if the lead singer didn't sound like Frankie Valli, Mike Love, or John Lennon, at least he didn't sound like Perry Como.

Overseeing the mayhem was an agitated Mr. Carver. He had given his say-so to the band and was now regretting it. He'd originally said, "Under no circumstances." But the student council had steadily worn him down until he'd caved. He stood in suit and tie on the opposite side of the gym, as far from the rockers as possible, and nervously stroked his chin, wondering what might go wrong. Normally reserved, he had been thrown for a loop by the pig incident, and he would be happy when the dance was over so he could resume the hunt.

The gym was filling rapidly now. Soon, student council president Jennifer Savio would step up to the microphone and announce the first bid dance. These ten reserved dances—spread throughout the evening—were to be coordinated with the slow numbers, a concession by the student leaders to the traditional way of doing things.

John and Michelle, happy as always in each other's company, watched some of their brave classmates attempt to stomp their way through the "Monster Mash."

"Not exactly a graveyard smash, is it?" The voice from close behind them belonged to Jeff, and the couple turned to greet him. On his arm was a blond-haired, blue-eyed beauty named Ingrid Johansson.

"Hello, Jeff," said Michelle.

"Hello, kids. You know Ingrid, right? Ingrid, this is John and Michelle."

The fact was that everyone knew Ingrid. With her fair skin and bright smile, she was one of the most sought-after goddesses in the school. Jeff had come through again, his rugged looks and bad-boy image a magnet for girls of substance who wanted to stretch their horizons for an evening. Her ultra-conservative Swedish parents would never allow her to date such a boy, but for her to meet up accidentally with him at a dance . . . well, her folks wouldn't have to know.

"Hi, Ingrid," said John, extending his hand to her.

"Hello, John. I was sorry to hear about your accident."

"Thank you."

She turned to Michelle. "You're the new girl, right?" It was true. Most of the others had grown up together. Michelle, like Jeff, would always be "new."

"Yes," said Michelle. "I came a few months ago."

"This is hysterical," laughed Jeff, and they all turned their attention to the dance floor. There, the dancers resembled Lucy Ricardo in the wine vat, stomping clumsily along to the beat.

"Look at Petey," said John, pointing out his nemesis to them.

Petey O'Neal looked like a chicken undergoing electrocution, his skinny body jerking spasmodically up and down. He was completely out of step with his partner, a girl twice his height. And, to add insult to apparent injury, his sport coat was too tight, his tie was too long, and his pants were too short.

And then Michelle noticed something the others had missed. Flashing back to the rubber snake, the lies spread about her mother, and the assault on John's ice cream soda, she waited patiently for the song to end and took her revenge.

As the smattering of applause died down, Michelle raised her voice so she could be easily heard. "Hey, Petey, did you forget to zip up?"

The boy froze on the dance floor. He looked down at the front of his pants.

So did everyone else.

Laughter cascaded across the crowded gym as Petey, hands cupped over his crotch, rushed out the door. He wasn't spotted the rest of the night.

John stared in awe at Michelle. "I can't believe you just did that."

"Why not?" she smiled sadistically. "It settles the score before I leave."

"Leave where?"

"School. We're graduating in a few days, remember?"

"Yeah," said John, confused now, "but we'll see him in high school this fall."

"Unfortunately. C'mon, it's a slow number. Let's dance."

Officially, it was bid number one. And, according to her pocket-sized book, a boy named John Belson had requested this dance. He had also signed up for bid numbers four, six, and ten.

Setting one of his crutches by the wall, he leaned on the other and, helped by Michelle, settled uneasily at the very edge of the dance floor far away from his peers. The last thing he wanted was for someone to bump into him and knock him to the floor. If that happened, he might as well join Petey in the land of losers.

He looked into Michelle's face. She smiled reassuringly, and everything seemed right with the world again. Balanced by her arms, he moved in a slow, rhythmic square. Momentarily at ease, the tension drained from his body. He smiled back at her.

John had dreamed of this moment his entire life. He held a girl he cared about awkwardly in one arm, and he knew he had found real love. Despite his injury, he felt no pain. He could have slow danced until dawn.

The night moved along. John watched several boys take turns escorting his girl onto the floor. Twinges of jealousy tweaked him from time to time, especially when another guy made her laugh with a clever, offhand remark. But, sensing his frustration, Michelle would wink at him as if to say, "Don't worry. He's not that funny. I'm only being polite."

For some reason, the hardest dance to watch from the sidelines was bid number seven. Jeff Womack held her tightly—too tightly, thought John—and they moved in unison, smoothly and effortlessly, like Astaire and Rogers. John felt sweat slide down the back of his neck and gather at his collar. He became suddenly nauseous. If any two people had a common bond, it was those two. He supposed, in this moment of anxiety, that Jeff and she would make a better couple, that alienation and loneliness would draw them instinctively to each other. But what of *his* loneliness? No, he was not going to give this seed a chance to grow. Time to cut in.

He angrily tucked his crutches under his armpit and started to move forward.

"I was right, wasn't I?"

John, startled out of his self-inflicted fury, turned to look into the face of Mr. Carver, who had sidled up beside him. "Huh?"

"I said that I was right, wasn't I? Remember way back at the start of the school year when I told you that you might be inclined to fall in love with some sparkling young lady? Well, I've been keeping my eye on you, Mr. Belson. I've seen the way you look at her. And might I add that you have very good taste?"

John blushed.

"Oh, don't be embarrassed. The staff is happy for you, and so am I."

John was dumbfounded. It had never occurred to him that his teachers might have been observing his interaction with Michelle. Or giving their collective blessing.

"Well, I'll leave you now. The dance is over, and I'm sure your friend Mr. Womack meant no harm."

John stared at Mr. Carver in amazement. "You mean . . . ?"

"I just thought it would be better for everyone if you didn't let your emotions get the best of you."

A flood of gratitude swept over John. "Thank you. Thank you, sir. I appreciate it. I really do."

Mr. Carver smiled. "Enjoy the rest of the dance, son." He turned away.

"Oh, Mr. Carver," said John, "I want you to know something else."

"What's that?"

"There were only three pigs."

***

The walk that John suggested wasn't a long one. Just across the moonlit field to the play equipment at the adjacent elementary school. The couple sat on the swings. Michelle removed her shoes and dragged her bare feet through the soft sand. They didn't talk for a long time. Finally, John broke the silence.

"I know you're leaving."

"How?"

"I'm not stupid. You didn't want to talk about this summer. Just one last night of fun. Oh, and your comment about getting even with Petey before you left."

Michelle stood and turned to face John. He was staring at the ground. She placed her fingers beneath his chin and slowly raised his head until their eyes met.

"I'm sorry. We're moving to live with my aunt in Colorado. She's set my mom up with a really good job."

"How long have you known?"

"About two weeks."

John paused. "When were you planning on telling me?"

"I'm not sure."

"What were you waiting for?"

"I didn't want to hurt you. No, that's not right. I didn't want to hurt *us*." Tears welled up in Michelle's eyes. "I don't want to leave you."

John stood on his good foot and wrapped his arms around her waist. He leaned in.

Their second—and last—kiss was much like the first, warm and tender. It didn't carry the promise of the first one, but it meant just as much.

"I love you," said John.

"I love you too," Michelle answered.

For the next few minutes, they stood still, entwined in an embrace, as if by doing so they could stop the earth from spinning on its axis and freeze the moment. Little did they realize they had done just that. For as their lives moved forward, the memory of the first time they fell in love would stay with them forever.

"You'll write?"

"John . . ."

"Maybe?"

"Maybe."

She broke away first, bending down and retrieving her shoes. He reached down for his crutches.

"We'll be fine," she said.

"I hope so."

There was an awkward pause.

"What is it?" asked Michelle.

"I believe, if you look in your bid book, you'll see that I requested dance number ten."

"Then we'd better hurry."

And so, as the band stumbled through a passable version of Gerry and the Pacemakers' "Don't Let The Sun Catch You Crying," John Belson and Michelle Watson clung to each other and wept softly. Still young, they did not yet comprehend that, when the dance ended, the music of their separate lives would play on forever like a sunshine symphony.

CPSIA information can be obtained at www.ICGtesting.com
Printed in the USA
BVOW07s1314220115

384512BV00001B/9/P